AS GOOD AS DEAD AS GO
GOOD AS DEAD AS GOOD
D AS DEAD AS G [barcode] S0-DQX-033 D
DEAD AS GOOD AS DEAD
D AS GOOD AS DEAD AS G
GOOD AS DEAD AS GOOD
D AS DEAD AS GOOD AS D
DEAD AS GOOD AS DEAD
D AS GOOD AS DEAD AS GO
GOOD AS DEAD AS GOOD
D AS DEAD AS GOOD AS D
DEAD AS GOOD AS DEAD
D AS GOOD AS DEAD AS GO
GOOD AS DEAD AS GOOD
D AS DEAD AS GOOD AS DE
DEAD AS GOOD AS DEAD A
D AS GOOD AS DEAD AS GO
OOD AS DEAD AS GOOD A
D AS DEAD AS GOOD AS DE
DEAD AS GOOD AS DEAD A
D AS GOOD AS DEAD AS GO
OOD AS DEAD AS GOOD A
OOD AS DEAD AS GOOD A

AS GOOD AS DEAD

(a cautionary tale)

STAN ROGAL

PEDLAR PRESS | TORONTO

ACKNOWLEDGEMENTS
The publisher wishes to thank the Canada Council for the Arts and the Ontario Arts Council for their generous support of our publishing program.

LIBRARY AND ARCHIVES CANADA
CATALOGUING IN PUBLICATION

Rogal, Stan, 1950-
　　As good as dead : a cautionary tale / Stan Rogal.
-- 1st ed.

ISBN 978-1-897141-16-8

I. Title.

PS8585.O391A8 2007　　　C813'.54
C2007-905380-7

First Edition

EDITED for the press by Ken Sparling
COVER ART Jacquie Jacobs
DESIGN Zab Design & Typography, Winnipeg

Printed in Canada

THE CANADA COUNCIL | LE CONSEIL DES ARTS
FOR THE ARTS | DU CANADA
SINCE 1957 | DEPUIS 1957

ONTARIO ARTS COUNCIL
CONSEIL DES ARTS DE L'ONTARIO

Fear of power invisible, feigned by the mind, or imagined from tales publicly allowed, [is called] RELIGION; not allowed [is called] SUPERSTITION. There is no _real_ difference between religion and superstition; all religion is sheer superstition. And the only meaningful difference between religions is political.

– THOMAS HOBBES (1588-1679)

Advertising is a vast, military operation openly and brashly intended to conquer the human spirit. The advertiser is a manipulator, yes. He plays around with human beings as if they were pigment. He smears us.

– MARSHALL MCLUHAN

The structure is episodic; the hero moves through a sequence of experiences, each one complete as a short narrative, yet the whole is given unity by the continuity of the central figure, and significance by the clearly stated objective behind the hero's journey.

– EDWARD BOND

1

lasciate ogni speranza voi ch'entrate:
All hope abandon ye who enter here

"Jack lay down obscure for the last time in his life. The ringing
. phone woke him the next morning and he was famous."

So said Joyce Johnson about Jack Kerouac when *On the Road*
hit the stands way back when, and what did he think, how did
he feel, did his hat size enlarge, did he wear his shirt differently
or a different colour, did he put his pants on right leg then left
whereas prior the opposite was true, or both legs at a time, did
he switch from Tokay to Beaujolais, from Bud to Brewer's Best
Wheat, from pork chops to T-bone steaks, was there a wiggle
in his walk, a giggle in his talk, or was there nothing out of the
ordinary; the same-old-same-old, *except* (perhaps) in the eyes of
others, yes? Or no?

And is it (has it always been) the same experience or feeling
for everyone, anyone, I wonder, who is magically, majestically,
dragged up from the lower depths of obscurity, yanked out
from the bowels of anonymity, plucked free from the pits of
mundanity and thus put on display as a *somebody*, a name, a

character, a personality, a celebrity, even, a *star* – why not? – to be recognized and reckoned with, sought after for views and opinions on politics, abortion, the death penalty, global warming, world finances, the status of the artist in today's society, disenfranchised youth, violence in the streets, pop culture, immigration policies, the war on drugs, the war on terror, the music scene, choice of toothpaste, brand of deodorant, flavour of ice cream, extraterrestrials, is reality TV really real, will the Jays win the pennant, is there a God, does my butt look big in these pants, and so on and so forth, yes? Or no?

No matter that one has grown accustomed to living in their own pale skin, accustomed to occupying their own tightly closeted (and safe!) milieu; that one has grown accustomed to a certain manner, *vis-à-vis*, how one is met and treated by others; how one meets and treats others: family, friends, acquaintances, lovers, possible lovers, partners, ex-partners, co-workers, strangers on the street, in a bar, surly waiters or waitresses, taxicab drivers, government officials, telemarketers, police officers, Girl Guide cookie peddlers, punks, neo-Nazi skinheads, left-wing fascists, Bible freaks, Martha Stewart wannabes or don't wannabes, arrogant sons-of-bitches who believe that the sun rises and sets on them alone, that their shit don't stink; scaredy-cats, religious pamphleteers, zealots of all sorts pushing faith, pills, exercise, caution, low fat, high fat, free love, chastity, technology, demonic democracy, vitamin supplements, unsightly hair removal, unnatural additives, breast expanders, thigh reducers, tummy tuckers, lip puckers, oat bran enemas, combination microwave oven/hair dryer/salad tosser/ skin exfoliator, the almighty dollar, muggers, panhandlers (hey – did you hear the one about the filthy decrepit disabled babbling schizophrenic who was raking in close to five hundred bucks a day begging loose change on street corners, *boo hoo*, and who each afternoon shed those false weeds at precisely quitting time, packed it all into the trunk of a spiffy new Lexus and drove home to a jazzy house in the Beaches for a chilled glass of Pinot Grigio and a plate of raw oysters? Yeah, me too! One bad apple spoiling the bunch, admitting there is a problem and many who are deserving, needing, stuck out there in all manner of cold-cruel-world foul weather, every levelled government turned a blind eye, myself in no great shit shape offering a coin here and there 'cause what else to do? my ex-wife relating a story of one guy asking her for seventeen cents to get home on the subway, her counting it out in front of him, him saying: *are you kidding me, lady, or what?* – she wasn't), bare naked ladies, little old ladies parcelled down for Christmas attempting to cross busy streets shouting, "Fucking asshole," at the unaware louts driving late model four-wheel-drive SUVs on cellphones drinking name-brand Styrofoam coffees reading *National Enquirers* with babies on their laps splashing all and sundry with filthy slush (and do you assist them or ignore them [the little old ladies, not the asshole drivers]; pretend you didn't see?), children, pets, strays, a herd of rampaging raging water buffaloes, bull elephants, rats in spats and suspenders, cockroaches in Gap gear, vending machines that fail to work or fail to work properly or give incorrect change or no change, pencil sharpeners that don't, unbreakable glass that does (remember the shit-for-brains stockbroker? lawyer? insurance agent? whoever, who threw himself against his office window to prove either its indestructibility or his stupidity, we're not sure, the jury still out on that one, and plummeted thirty-nine Hitchcockian floors to his urban legend death and, no matter Aristotle's: "The end of man is an action, not a thought," this is fucking ludicrous behaviour for a grown man), men of the cloth with feet of clay, athletes who can't get it up, politicians who can't get it down, *the unacknowledged legislators of the world*, for all you Shelley fans out there, in other words: the gamut; the entire nine yards; the complete ball of earwax.

No matter (in addition) that one has been toiling away

relentlessly for years, even decades, at one's craft, the phenomenon of recognition is experienced as immediate and spontaneous whether the perspective is situated outside the person, that is, the world at large, or from within, meaning: walls are torn down, ceiling and roof ripped asunder, floors pried out from beneath and one is suddenly exposed and floating sixty naked bloody feet above the ground for all to see and critique – Jack felt struck as if by the proverbial bolt out of the blue: lightning (or, in deference to Jack's own preferred metaphor: a blast of flaming Roman candle, complete with sulphurous odour).

He had been touched by the wing of an angel or by the hand of God or by the hem of the gods or by the belly of Buddha or by the sword tip of Allah or by the fire of Mohammed or by the flowing silky hair of Gaia or by the golden mandibles of the sacred scarab of Isis or by the rolling thunderball of Thor or by the milky white teat of Sheela-na-Gig or by the roiling crashing waters of the seven seas or by the four fast-moving winds or, most likely, by the fickle finger of fate, of Fates, ('cause with every action occurs an equal and opposite reaction [so somebody said: Euclid? Archimedes? Gretzky?] yes? Or no? And, also, what goes up must come down and to everything, *turn, turn, turn,* there is a season, *turn, turn, turn,* and the road to hell is paved with good intentions and bad inventions and blessed be the meek for they shall be trod upon with enormous jackboots [get the pun?] and not with a bang but a whimper and the spinning wheel goes 'round and 'round and the painted ponies [as well] go up and down and cream sinks, my friend, to the very freaked out bottom, eventually, while every other *detritus dreck doo-doo* rises to the top and floats with careless abandon and is, if not embraced, at least assimilated into the community at large, and every other half-baked cliché automatically comes to bear and for good reason or reasons which are often left unspoken and of which we remain more or less unaware.

More or less. More or less, though there are hints; there are signs; there are tiny voices in the back of the head, in the gut, in the wilderness crying out, if only we were willing, if only we were able, if only we had the wherewithal to make the effort, take the time, but we are caught up in the swirl and not waving but drowning, pal. Drowning, pure and simple.)

Yes? Or no?

Face it, once the star-making machinery is put in motion and begins its grind there is no turning back (Euclid, Archimedes and/or the great Gretzky notwithstanding).

"Is no turning back!" Exclamation mark and quotations, full stop. The bathwater parts and accommodates. Eureka!

Jack Kerouac was no longer. He was: JACK KEROUAC, writer of *On the Road* and newly appointed (anointed) spokesperson for the *beat* generation – whether he wanted it or not – complete (again; still) with exclamation mark and quotations, full stop, and death to any and all innocents who dared attempt to spanner the works. Though no one did, and why would they? Rather stick out a thumb and hop aboard. After all, if not a god himself, at least raised to the level of literary lion, an icon, a *cause célèbre* meant to be praised, feted, honoured (almost worshipped [and in some circles, smallish, yes, worshipped]): *Deo gratias, Deo gratias, Deo gratias...*

Out of the frying pan, into the fire. What to do except strap yourself in, grit your teeth, hang on tight and boot it to no destination no place no where. What did it matter? The thing was: Drive, he said! Keep moving, goddamn it! Gun the bitch! And whatever else you do, don't ease up, don't stop, 'cause you never know what that black and white dot is that's creeping up in the rear-view mirror or what it's capable of accomplishing.

Poor Jack.

Poor, poor Jack. *De mortuis nil nisi bonum:* say nothing but good of the dead. (Latin, right? Another defunct tongue chock full of life. *In vino veritas.* Today's soft and fuzzy, user-friendly populace simply translates: in wine there is truth. Sounds nice, sounds refreshing, sounds like we discover something within the wine: flavour, bouquet, richness, beauty, joy and so on. The message? Drinking wine will enhance your life. Go out and purchase a bottle or two now. Buy a case. Digging deeper, going behind the thin facade, we scratch out a further, possibly pernicious meaning: truth is told under the influence of liquor. In other words: watch out! A few quick smashes and God knows what will come flying out of one's mouth. Just as easily 'Take this job and shove it!' as toeing the company line; just as easily 'Fuck you and your mother!' as offering the expected banal apology. A horse of a very different colour altogether and one which many would choose not to mount. I can see the winemakers now, their purple legs trembling in the vats, the sales graphs nose-diving. Not that it bothers me. I raise a glass: to Truth, in all its varied guises, disguises and manifestations.

De mortuis nil nisi bonum: say nothing but good of the dead.

Fair enough. I have nothing but good things to say. Of the dead or otherwise (the living dead being an exception here, you understand, and deserving nothing less than a stake driven mercilessly through the heart to end not only *their* endless misery and suffering but *ours* as well). *De profundis:* out of the depths. Surely. Dragged. By the bootstraps; by the short hairs. Out of his depth and in over his head. Famous. For a fleeting Warholian minute (or was that fifteen minutes? Or fifteen seconds?) As someone once said (and hasn't someone once said [an old Greek or Roman probably] just about everything that can, should or needs to be said, repeatedly, backwards and forwards?): No mind? No matter.

Or was that Woody Allen?

Alas, poor Jack! I knew him, Horatio: a man of infinite jest, of most excellent fancy: he hath borne me on his back a thousand times...

And now? Now it was my turn at the wheel; my turn to wake

up one fine morning and be whisked off to the stars, though via a more circuitous route, for, in this day and age of *stark and unloving actualities* a work of literature, a novel, simply doesn't cut it. If it isn't all net or the long ball or a putt from sixty feet or a slapshot from the blue line or some such other nifty spoiled *sport,* or a pop song sung by an anorexic teen or boy band, or inflated titties, or a muscle-bound *schlock* movie, you're lucky if you make it into the back pages of the Sunday book supplement of the local daily.

Such was my fortune that, after a year of taking up derelict space on a few (very few) bookstore shelves across Canada and the US, a Big Shot (simply going by the numbers, here, no real personal knowledge at this juncture) Hollywood film producer was handed my novel by a secretary who just happened to be given a review copy (though not reviewed, necessarily, rather likely stuck unceremoniously into a plastic bag along with others until enough to trade in for the latest John Grisham, the latest Stephen King or a cholesterol free cookbook or how-to or twelve step program or...

Bitter? Maybe a tad bitter, maybe simply realistic given the *Age* where money affords press and most reviewers' hands are tied or else they've given up; caved in to the pressure and are content to drone on about the top ten *ad infinitum, ad nauseum* for promise of a paycheque and pension plan) by a new beau who had a friend who had an acquaintance who had a cousin who just happened to be strolling along a side street in a seedy section of downtown LA and who just happened to pick up the review copy nonchalantly as a ruse, as a way of trying to look like he or she belonged, picked it up quite accidentally, in plain truth, from a used book bin, paid the couple of discounted bucks, then skedaddled out of there, fearing the worst, and sauntered into an upscale coffee shop, a *brasserie,* perhaps a Starbucks, and actually read it or part of it or skimmed through it or caught the blurb, maybe, who knows, over a double grande caffe latte light with cinnamon sprinkles and a chocolate biscotti, and was somewhat taken or marginally impressed by its filmic quality and passed it along and passed it along and passed it along until finally it was plunked into the above-mentioned secretary's hot little hand, and killing time over tuna salad lunches – no dressing (watching her weight, *donchyaknow*) – and cigarette breaks, managed to motor through (and as much to placate the arrogant bastard boss who was ranting [as usual] about the lack of decent material [he who was known for producing low brow blow 'em up good *bang-bang* car chase fiery inferno *chop-chop* exploding chainsaw massacre monsters from Mars *scream-scream* blood and gore hide the sausage stick a magnum in the mouth pull the trigger splatter the brains across the upholstery the glass the other occupants of the car juvenile tits and ass blockbusters] as to promote my novel, the secretary slaps him with it [though not really *it*, the book, but a down-and-dirty synopsis complete with extra large buttered popcorn, soft drink and a fucking egg roll]).

"Brilliant!" he says. "We'll do it!"

In sorry sad fact, it may not have happened this way at all. Even in part. It likely didn't. I mean, how could it? The story is ridiculous, preposterous, totally unbelievable. To be honest, I have no idea as to the actual sequence of events. This is pure conjecture on my part, a romanticization (now, there's a ten dollar word) drawn from a thousand bad movie plots and a thousand more poorly written accounts about how so-and-so did such-and-such and Lana Turner being discovered in Schwab's wearing the famous sweater or Jimmy Cagney firing "You dirty rat" or Humphrey Bogart mumbling "Play it again Sam" or Jane Russell sporting Howard Hughes's aerodynamic push-up bra (what?) in the poster shot for *The Outlaw* circa 1941 (Jane quoted as saying: "Howard may be a genius at designing airplanes, but he has a lot to learn about women's undergarments."), or this-that-and-the-other-thing that never really occurred but makes great copy and is the very stuff of further urban legends.

Though Marilyn Monroe was definitely not wearing underwear when that subway train steamed between her legs and blew her skirt up around her ears. There is no question. I've seen the photos. Or imagine I have, ha ha.

OK, what is sure and no disputing (whatever the circumstances) is that the discovery was followed by a million dollar feature film contract causing a meteoric rise in popularity (not in me *per se*, at least not immediately, but in the book, not so accidentally titled *The Long Drive Home*).

And so, another road movie, another buddy movie, another story of coincidences and failed opportunities and lost loves and sexual intrigues and a shootout at the OK corral (metaphorically speaking) and a cross-dressing salesman and a suicidal lawyer and a little girl with a photographic memory and a mother who's into self-mutilation and a pair of troubled detectives with sexual identity issues and a cute dog set to sate the appetite of a purblind waiting public. 'Cause I wasn't about to kid myself. I knew that folks were buying the book *not* because of the writing, but because it was to be made into a big Hollywood extravaganza. I also knew (or highly suspected or had a hunch) that the movie, ultimately, would end as a great piece of stinking caca moved straight from big screen to DVD.

If I'm so lucky.

Picture already, as Hollywood is wont to do, the characters' ages lowered by ten or fifteen years, their features airbrushed, their bodies trimmed, their blemishes covered. Ben Affleck and Matt Damon as the two detectives who may or may not be gay (cut that immediately, yes? No doubt, the men straight as fucking arrows). The horsey-faced woman? Aaa, wrong! Replaced by Gwyneth Paltrow. The paunchy lawyer? Aaa, wrong! Toss in a Baldwin brother, any Baldwin brother. The short, stocky female lead? Aaa, wrong again! Up the eye candy with busty *can't-act-her-way-out-of-a-beer-commercial* Salma Hayek. And forget the self-mutilation aspect, let's make the woman a cocaine freak, which is socially more acceptable and doesn't ruin the manicure.

I could go on, but why bother?

Did I care? Did it matter? Deep down, maybe, but on the surface one tends to think (I thought, at any rate): the door is open, jump in before it shuts and locks. Make some money, have some fun, relax for a change, enjoy your time in the limelight, establish yourself, so that next time (there is always the notion of a next time squirrelling around the brainpan, yes, whether misguided or not?) you can afford to call the shots. You can afford to maintain your integrity in the name of Art.

Right.

If that's what you want. Personally, I don't give a sweet damn about the movies. I go to them, I enjoy them, I have some critical appreciation of them, enough to separate the wheat from the chaff, you know? I have an objective eye and an educated opinion in terms of content and form, but I don't want to make them. I'm a writer. Moreover, I'm a poet, and even the novel (which I am proud of and believe works on many levels) was simply a way of attempting to earn a decent amount of money in order to buy time so that I might concentrate my efforts on the creation of another slim volume of verse.

How did it come about in the first place? My publisher's idea. It was sometime early March. We were getting together for drinks and dinner at Paupers Pub to discuss my latest poetry manuscript which he was going to print in the fall. Our meeting was set for eight o'clock. Kevin rolled in around nine-thirty, pie-eyed, pooched, plastered, gonzoed, snapped, ripped, smashed, blasted three sheets to the ever-lovin' wind. He'd been at an earlier gathering where one thing led to another and one drink led to another and another still. He sat down, unzipped his coat, removed gloves, scarf, baseball cap, and lit up a smoke (those days when there was a smoking section: no longer). I was working my way through a half-liter of Chilean red and Kevin called for a pint of Upper Canada lager. We joked, laughed, made the usual chit-chat: Hey, how are ya? What's up? Whaddya say? How's things? Where've ya been? What happened to you? And so on until the story of "how I got shit-faced" eventually came out.

Kevin was in a fine mood. Pissed to the gills and in a fine mood. After a couple of drinks I handed him my manuscript which he took, gave a cursory glance (and how much or how well could he see, I hadn't the foggiest), folded in half and fumbled into his coat pocket.

"Vic," he said. "I love your poetry. You know I love your poetry. And I'm going to publish this. OK? That's settled. That's agreed upon. That's old news; history. You understand? But, you know what? You know what I'm really waiting for and what I wish to encourage?"

I smiled and shrugged. "No. What?"

"I wanna publish your novel."

"My novel? I don't have a novel."

"You don't have a novel? You don't have a novel?" Kevin drank his beer and lit another cigarette. "You have a novel. Everyone has a novel. Every writer, especially, has a novel. Inside you, inside your pen, you have a novel. The idea of a novel, yes? The kernel. The spark. You do, don't you?"

"I guess I have an idea."

What I had were a few small bits and pieces that had the possibility of becoming one large piece; perhaps a novel, though more likely a short story, or several short stories.

"You see? What did I say, hmm? It's inside you, all you have to do is sit down and put it on paper."

"Yeah." I pondered this for a second, what he said: *That's all you have to do.* "Sure, I mean...wasn't it James Dickey who stated, 'Any idiot can write a novel'? I certainly fit that category."

I laughed. Kevin remained serious.

"Bingo. What I'm telling you; what I'm saying. You see? Eh? A goddamn novel. Dickey, he knocked off *Deliverance* and presto! Instant fame and fortune. Kerouac, in two weeks, on a single roll of typing paper: *On the Road*. Yes? Poof! Overnight success. Right? Right? Goddamn right. I can't guarantee that'll happen to you, right? But I can tell you that more copies of novels sell than collections of poems. Any goddamn novel, any time, anywhere."

I could understand Kevin's argument. He was a relatively young guy, early thirties, who decided (for some strange, crazed and obviously masochistic reason) a few years back, say four or five, to start up his own alternative press, Vigilante Editions, which somehow continues to exist through the grace of God, government grants, volunteers and spotty book sales. On a shoestring, basically. A very thin, frayed shoestring. To be fair, he had printed two of my poetry collections already, which, although garnering decent reviews, failed to rouse the poetry-buying public (if such an animal roams the aisles in any great number anymore, which I doubt). In a funny way, I owed him. Besides, it wasn't that I was against writing a novel *in principle*, simply that I couldn't see the point of slaving away for months or years on a project that would never see the light of day. At least my poems appeared in literary magazines and anthologies and Kevin had been, so far, amenable to putting out a book here and there. What's that phrase? Better a slim possibility than a... than a... Can't remember. *Something something...* impossibility.

Whatever. I had always considered the reality of my ever writing and publishing a novel to be a total impossibility. On so many levels. For me, it had become a non-issue. Really. It wasn't merely below the radar, it didn't even exist beyond the screen.

"So, if I write a novel...you're saying...?"

"I'll print it in next year's season. A goddamn novel. The poems this year, the novel next. Hmm?"

"You know, if I do write a novel, if I'm able, it won't be a four hundred page epic about growing up Protestant in a small Canadian town with a cancerous mother and abusive father? Or exploring my identity as an immigrant or displaced person or disenfranchised youth? Or coming to terms with my sexuality?"

"It's your novel. Write what you want. I love your work. I want more people to read it. So long as it's over one hundred and thirty-five pages, that's all I ask."

"Are you kidding me?"

Kevin shook his head, no. "The granting bodies, bless them. Minimum one hundred and thirty-five pages, otherwise..." He mimicked slitting his throat with a finger and made a sound. "Ccckkk." We laughed and drank up. The waiter came by. "Another wine, another beer and two Jack Daniels."

"They've checked out the classics, I suppose, counted the pages," I said.

"I suppose."

"Camus' *The Fall*," I go. "One hundred twenty pages."

"Not really a classic."

"Voltaire's *Candide*, one hundred seven pages."

"Ancient history."

"Marguerite Duras' *The Lover*, one hundred twenty-two pages, large print."

"They never would've heard of her."

"Sheila Watson's *The Double Hook*, one hundred thirty-four pages."

"Under the wire. Hey – have you ever noticed that when we talk about male writers it's always last names only and when we talk about female writers it's both names? I mean, you'd never say, that novel by Woolf or that novel by Atwood. It's always *Virginia* Woolf, *Margaret* Atwood."

"Yeah. The same in bed. You're having sex, you're fucking, and they want to be called by their Christian names. What is that?"

"They think it's more intimate; more personal," said Kevin. "They want to feel different from any other woman you've banged. And if you want to call them all *honey*, you better be in the supermarket buying milk and eggs 'cause it won't cut it between the sheets."

"Right." I recall a buddy of mine in a former life, a real pickup artist, who did just that – called them all honey – so as not to make a mistake during moments of intimacy, he said. Once, during a bit of afternoon delight, a woman grabbed him by both ears while he was still riding her: *what's with this honey bullshit? you can't remember my name, can you?* She was a stripper with big tits, bad teeth and a temper. They were nose to nose. He thought she was going to tear his head off. Instead, she laughed, hoisted her hips, gave her pussy a squeeze, *Fucker*, she said, and got him to come. As he collapsed on top of her, she ran her nails down the sides of his buttocks. *I been with you four times, you shit*, and she dug her nails, raked him asshole to shoulder blades, then tossed him to the floor. *You explain that to your cunt wife, huh!* She jumped to her feet, wiggled into bra and panties, slung her high heels over a shoulder, grabbed personal belongings, knocked things over, smashed stuff: lamps, glasses, bottles, barrelled out of the room; exited stage left, more or less naked. My buddy lay bleeding on the carpet, half wishing she had torn his head off. Half wishing he was dead.

"Eggs?" I went on. "Bataille's *Story of the Eye*, one hundred three pages."

"Pornography."

"Pynchon's *Gravity's Rainbow*, one hundred nineteen pages."

"Yeah, right. Pynchon doesn't write a book that can't be used as a weapon or a doorstop later. Nice try, but you're stuck with it. One-three-five."

"Gotcha." I pushed at the stained coaster with a finger.

Wait! I thought. I remember now! Better a possibility that appears impossible than an impossibility that appears possible.

That's it, isn't it? Isn't it? Better a...better a...a possibility... than...than a...an...impossibility... No. What did I say? Was that it? Shite! Never mind. Forget it. The wine's gone to my head. I've had it. Another time, another day, maybe. The file will resurface, but not here; not now.

The drinks arrived. Kevin raised his glass and grinned. "To success."

"To success." We tossed back the bourbon. It made a lovely slow burn down my throat and in my belly. It felt good. I felt good.

We closed the place down and took our separate ways home. Both on foot, both of us higher than kites, the cool March air roughing the cheeks and doing its best to clear the smoke out of my lungs. There would be a headache tomorrow. Tonight, I was dancing: I was going to be a novelist. All I had to do was sit down and write the goddamn thing.

That's all I had to do.

And so, I did.

What is it they say; someone said? A Scotsman? The best laid plans...the best *made* plans...of mice and men do oft a'gone a'glee. Something like that (and what sort of plans do mice make and are they artists? Do they have insufferable, inflated egos? Do they seek fame? Even once dropped into the maze are they hoping to come out the other end as stars? Are they as crazy and self-centred as humans or are they only after the cheese, man, where's the cheese, gimme the cheese?) which roughly translated means that no matter what you do or try to do you never know, it's never sure, and it could all blow up in your face.

Murphy's law: whatever can go wrong will go wrong.

Precisely. And what was it some other bright light added? Oh yeah: Murphy was an optimist.

At any rate, I was seemingly on my way. Sales soared, the

money rolled in, the PR boys and girls had me booked solid into every minor and major venue, either reading, signing or just plain hyping product. And it is precisely here that the real journey begins, for who knew what manner of creature was to fly out once the Pandora's box had been unlocked and sprung opened?

2

Novus homo: A new man raised from obscurity

The telephone.

It's around nine in the a.m. I'm unshaved, unshowered, in sweats and slippers, fixing myself a little breakfast. Nothing too complicated: two slices of buttered rye toast on a blue plate, containers of strawberry jam and peanut butter on the table beside, an unpeeled banana, cuppa fresh coffee in a mug that says *Pisces* and *who could it be? who could it be?*

Not too early for a call, simply too early for most folks I know, who are mainly writer/actor/artist types working as caterers, bartenders, table servers, dishwashers till the wee hours in order to support their habit, so likely still sawing logs in bed. On the reverse side of that same dull coin, into construction or office temping, ducking out for an hour or two here or there to attend auditions, take classes, so already at work and in no mood or right state of mind to be socializing, merely mainline the caffeine and count off the hours, minutes, seconds, until able to punch the clock and skedaddle.

Which makes me hazard to guess: someone wanting to sell me a newspaper subscription? But sir, how can you possibly refuse? What part of this exceptionally fine offer don't you understand? Let me repeat so that it might sink into your ignorant thick skull. The first month is absolutely *gratis*, FREE, after that we're practically giving it away. You can order seven days a week, just weekends, just weekdays, every other day, every third day, one day a week...it is up to you; your decision. You are under no obligation to continue beyond the initial thirty-day FREE trial period, at which point you can cancel either by phone, by letter, by e-mail or by logging on to our convenient Web site. If you should decide to continue your subscription after the FREE trial period (and why wouldn't you?), there is absolutely nothing to sign; no contract of any kind; the fees are withdrawn directly from your bank account or charged to your credit card and, again, you can change your service or cancel at any time. Going away for a weekend? a week? a month? Don't worry! We will adjust to your schedule at no extra charge. There are absolutely no hidden costs. No salesperson will ever approach either you or your family directly. The icing on the cake? The *pièce de résistance* (that's *French*, you uncultured, uneducated shit for brains)? Your name will be entered in a draw to win a trip for two to sunny Barbados, excluding hotel, food, drinks and applicable taxes. To top it off, we deliver the paper to your goddamn door, fer Chrissakes, by seven in the morning or four in the afternoon, again up to you, whatever is most suitable, *guaranteed* or your delivery person is flogged, shot, hung, quartered and your subscription cheerfully extended another month. Are you with me so far? Huh? This is ground control to Major Tom: Can you hear me? Have I made contact? Houston? The lights are on, is anyone home? Hello? Hello? Is there a problem? Have I not made myself abundantly crystal clear? C'mon, work with me, work with me people. I'm dying here! Throw me a freaking bone! I mean, what are you? Crazy, stupid, illiterate, a fucking moron, can't you see I'm trying to scratch out a living?

Whassat, whassat? *I go.* What you say? Barbie dolls? Funkin' Wagnalls? Ernie Eves? You want I should scratch your bone? No way José. No falamos espagnol. No parlez. No sprechen-zie zilch paysan. Nada. You couscous. Capiche? Auf veeder zane. Avaunt, oh worm-faced fellow of the night!

Click!

A survey or opinion poll: what makes my whites whiter, my colours brighter? Where do I shop for toiletries, vitamins, handguns, crack cocaine?

Sorry?

Oh, did I say handguns and crack cocaine? I meant hardware and computer games.

Nice try sweetheart, I can spot a hawk from a handsaw, a Freudian slip from an entrapment any old day of the week (the joke where one guy says to the other: "That happened to me once – I wanted to say to my wife, 'Pass the cornflakes,' and instead said, 'You ruined my life, you fucking bitch, har har!'").

How good a job do I think the provincial government is doing: very good, good or reasonably good?

The provincial government sucks, I rage! The premier is in bed with the corporations, taking a four wood up the wah-zoo without a rubber! The MPPs are all former Nazi storm troopers turned used car salesmen intent on force feeding us lemons! The minister of the environment is a gas jockey for Exxon. The minister of education...

Sorry sir, that's not a category.

Hey, wait a goldarn minute! I was just getting started! And why stop at the provincial government? The mayor is a third-rate clown complete with cheap red plastic nose, baggy pants, purple fright wig and a hard-on for WWF and the Spice Girls...

Click!

A tenth reminder from the dentist's office that my six

month checkup is currently fifteen months past?

I know, I know, and as soon as a rich relative pops off and I have the necessary exorbitant funds to pay for services rendered, I'll be there.

Are you trying to tell me that you don't have a dental plan? Because our records clearly show...

Gone with my ex-wife over two years ago. Please delete from your computer. As a matter of fact, don't call me, I'll call you, OK?

I'm sorry sir, we can't allow that. As a prized client, you are in our automated system, entitling you to our complete line of services, including friendly reminders and helpful tips. Did you floss today? Remember that your smiling teeth make a lasting first impression on friends and business associates, so it's up to you to do your best to make it a good one.

I'll make it a good one all right, how would you like five in the kisser?

Are you seeing someone else? Is that it?

C'est what?

Another dentist?

Another...?

Have you been unfaithful? Gone behind our backs for promise of coupons, sliding scale and a quick peek at naughty X-rays?

Now wait a pin pricking minute here...

A bit of the old drill and run, is that it? Is that your game? Never mind who gets hurt so long as your pearly whites are buffed and polished?

Why, I oughta...

Have a pleasant day, traitor.

I said hold on!

This has been a recording, a recording, a recording...

Rats, foiled again.

Click!

Upgrade my cable? Why? I don't watch the damn thing now except to drive myself crazy with the remote. Wasn't it Bruce Springsteen who sang way back in the seventies or eighties: "There's fifty-seven channels and nothin' on?" Except now, there's five hundred channels and nothing on. As an actor friend of mine is fond of repeating (and wasn't it Kafka who said: "Warnings not only bear repetition, they demand it!"?): "TV programs only exist to push product, and producers would be more than happy to show twenty-four straight hours of two dogs fucking if it sold an extra bag of potato chips."

The story of Charles Bukowski's girlfriend wanting a television and Buk saying no, no, no...it's nothin' but horse piss. Finally submitting to the pressure, he rents one for a trial period, turns it on and *whadyaknow* the first thing he encounters is David Lynch's *Eraserhead* and figures, hey, this is pretty good, maybe I was wrong. As if the producers knew, had it planned, 'cause after that it was flip, flip, flip...the stations mired in horse piss and still the box sits there, unused, attracting dust and flies, not even worth the bother to have it returned or the effort to chuck it out the goddamn window.

What was that lie they told us (you know who *they* are? *They*, *them* and *the others*? The ones *outside* and *beyond* who make the rules and who don't merely tug the strings but wrap them tightly around ankles and throats then *twist* so as to control completely), when the Garden of Cable Delights still appeared fresh, innocent, golden and there was nary a sign of a fork-tongued slithering serpent, poisonous or otherwise? You'd pay one low monthly fee for cable and enjoy 24-hour-a-day, commercial-free viewing? That was it, yes? That was the promise – heaven on earth.

Yeah, right, now pull the other leg And the middle one while you're at it.

Hissssss...

Oh, but sir, there is commercial-free cable, you simply have to pay, pay, pay, pay, pay, through the nose, over and above the shitty basic package we provide that you don't want in the first place and have to accept anyway.

Uh-huh. You know, normally I get kissed before I get fucked.

Excuse me?

Forget it.

Click!

Upgrade my telephone? Upgrade my insurance? Upgrade my Internet? Apply for a special line of credit for special customers? Purchase a half-acre lot of prime Florida swampland on easy terms over a ninety-nine year amortization plan no money down no payments till spring mortgage one quarter percentage point below bank rate no one turned down everyone qualifies includes a bonus pair of authentic alligator boots if you act now! It's only scant pennies a minute, a couple of dollars a day, a few buckaroos per month, a modicum of cash sterling per year...

I guess they never tried that brainteaser that poses: what would you rather have, a one lump sum of a million dollars or a penny doubled each second for a minute?

You do the math.

Click, click, click!

My racket? I work part-time as a door-to-door fundraiser, usually four nights a week, though it's flexible, three in the afternoon until ten or eleven at night by the time the money's counted and the paperwork is done, for Friends of the Ecology, an environmental group that lobbies business and government for changes in attitude and practice, like: "Stop shoving poisons down our throats before you kill us all, you bastards! Think of the children!"

Not exactly subtle, but as Woody Allen said in one of his movies (*Annie Hall? Manhattan?*): you want to stop the parade of neo-Nazi skinheads down Main Street USA, you don't write letters or publish articles of polite indignation, you roll up your sleeves, arrive with bricks and baseball bats and get down to it. I'm paraphrasing, but you get the drift.

A good cause, a terrific cause, though the wrong climate (pardon the pun) at the present moment, the environment not being a particularly sexy topic given recent world events: 9/11, terrorism, anthrax scares, SARS, monkeypox, our boys off fighting the good fight, one religion hacking the other to bits and eating their young, suicide bombers, is Britney Spears really a virgin? will we truly always have Paris? what about them Leafs? is it a chip or a cracker? *Whoa Nelly!* The economy reportedly in a mess no matter how much obscenely high record profits the major banks and corporations are stashing away (remember our miserable little penny? The lesson is not lost on the money mongers who want [and expect!] not simply interest, but interest on the interest, then interest on the interest on the interest and so on and so forth behaving as if resources, whether natural or otherwise, are endless – which they ain't, pal. Some one fine day the bottom falls out, the golden goose quacks and *cacks,* leaving nothing but a few mangy feathers and a bad smell). In the *mean* time (in between time), the skies open and the cancerous ultraviolet rays slice through like some beyond mythic hot-under-the-collar dragon spewing flames from both ends, scorching the earth, wreaking havoc with the weather, blighting the forests, boiling the oceans, generally cranking up the heat, and for most (that is, the populace at large), the predicament is met simply by an icy cold Corona *cerveza* with a wedge of lime, a pair of Gucci sunglasses, a slathering of number 45 sunscreen, a pat on the bum, a high-five and: "Nice tan, dude! And, oh so quick!"

Future so bright you gotta wear shades.

Ba-boom!

And how do our politicians respond, those vanguards of responsibility and public welfare? With Band-Aid solutions, naturally, preferring to cope short-term rather than long-term; preferring to focus on symptoms rather than causes. Air unbreathable? No problem – we'll fit you with a gas mask, complete with designer coloured straps and nifty maple leaf pattern to go with your wardrobe. Water undrinkable? We'll sell you bottled water. Imported, even. From France. *C'est si bon! la parapluie est un chien!* Can't afford public transit? Drive, you sons of bitches! Why do you think God provided us with cars? Too many poor people on the streets? We'll arrest the stinking reprobates and toss them in the pokey. Not enough money for the Arts? Get real jobs, you mewling left-wing pansy bloodsucking lazy fucks! (I mean, why stretch oneself when one maybe won't be around after four years in office, instead, take the pay raise, the guaranteed pension plan and *blah, blah, blah* drone on with catchphrases and rhetoric, right? Something about a trickle-down effect? Something about depending on the private sector and technology to *make-like-the-cavalry* and come to our rescue, save us all at the penultimate moment?)

Trickle-down effect my ass, for it is written: *more people in the world die of starvation than of all the wars and all the diseases combined.*

And not just underdeveloped nations but on our very own doorstep, in case you haven't looked out the window lately or had to stand in line at a food bank.

As for technology, what's it done for us in recent times ('us' being the favoured Ugly North Americans who comprise one tenth of the world's population but manage to consume ninety percent of the world's resources) except kept us living longer hooked up to the tube, one hand on the joy stick, the other wrapped around a six-pack of Ding Dongs?

Yeah, yeah.

Still (and through it and beside it all), pound on enough doors and you manage to encounter enough friendly concerned souls to scrape together enough filthy lucre to keep the organization if not happy at least up and running, plus get paid a few shekels yourself. Not much, though enough to cover the bills and keep stocked in pen, paper and ink-jet cartridges (along with the obligatory poet fare: hundred naked watt light bulb, cheese, crackers, bottle of cheap hooch). As well, you feel like you're doing something positive for the world at large.

"Think global, act local."

Sure, meanwhile most of the so-called underdeveloped world is stuck just fighting to survive, never mind afforded the luxury of time to consider change.

How did I end up working for Friends of the Ecology? A long, convoluted story involving a pulling up of stakes and a re-establishing in a new city, Vancouver to Toronto, all for the love of a woman, the romance long since drawn to a close, the marriage broken, the paperwork signed, sealed, delivered, the property (what little there was) divided, the rings tossed into back corners of separate drawers in separate abodes, the hearts on the mend, and what else to do with an M.A. in English except drive cab or sling beer or knock on strangers' doors in the middle of the night begging for money?

The telephone, the telephone.

"Hello."

"Vic?"

"Yeah. Kevin. What's up?"

"You want some good news? Even excellent news?"

"Love it."

"I arrive in the office this morning, turn on the computer, and, guess what?"

"What?"

"There's an e-mail from L A."

"Yeah?"

"It's from a film production company."

"O K."

"They want to shoot your novel."

"My novel?"

"They're offering a flat fee buyout of one million dollars. They do everything. They already sent a contract like the deal's done. And it is, so far as I'm concerned. Well? How do you feel? What do you think? Fantastic or what? It's fantastic, right?"

"Yeah. Fantastic. Am I to be involved in the adaptation?"

"No. You're invited to fly in and talk with the writers in case they have questions, which apparently they won't. You can sit in a few days on the set, all expenses paid, but it's their baby once we sign the bottom line."

"Do they want me to do anything?"

"Sure, you know – the usual. Be available for publicity shots, go on radio and TV shows, basically talk the movie up. It's all laid out in the contract. Basic, straightforward and...did I mention? A million bucks!"

"Free and clear, right? Up front? Not a million bucks less this, that and the toilet paper in the executive washroom? Five hundred grand for me and five hundred grand for the press; for you."

"Flat fee. Just you and the tax department. That's it."

"Are you sure we shouldn't be asking for a penny doubled each second over a sixty second period?"

"Are you kidding me?"

"Yeah."

"Oh. Good."

"And I don't do anything?"

"A few things. A couple of things. It's all in the contract. Anyway, you wrote the book, right? What more do you have to do? On the creative end, I mean. This other stuff...business, that's all. Schmoozefest. Travel, cocktail parties, lobster dinners, martinis with...whoever – Gwyneth, Ben, Tom. I don't know. Opening night ceremonies. Ribbon cutting, kiss mothers, shake babies, whatever. Tough job."

"OK. What's next? What do I do?"

"Haul ass in here and sign, my friend. Take a cab. My feeling is, they want this done yesterday. My feeling is, the movie is already made, it's playing in theatres everywhere, soon to be in a video store near you, *ka-ching, ka-ching!* The cash registers can't add the money quick enough. It's arriving in bags by the truckload."

"You think?"

"Who knows, who cares? A million bucks up front."

"I'm on my way."

Click!

So, this is it. The phone call. The beginning. I'm standing here unshaved, unshowered, smelling of B.O., in my sweats, slippers, a cuppa in my hand, toast grown cold upon the plate. No different. The banana remains unpeeled on the table, fer Chrissakes. Outside the window, the city is still shivering in the goddamn snow. Where is the romance? Do I call someone? Who do I call? My family's on the west coast and three hours time difference makes it six ten. My lady friend is married with children (yeah, I know, naughty boy, yet you rarely choose who you're going to be attracted to or fall in love with, it merely occurs and you are more pawn than king, so no attitude, no judgment, *thankyouverymuch*. Besides, it takes two to tango and she is not a happy camper, this to do with her husband, of course, the kids she loves, loves, loves to death and doesn't want to hurt in any way, shape or form, so, the wheels spin, kicking up lots of dirt and gravel and going nowhere fast) and who knows who might pick up the phone? Husband home, kid sick, mother visiting? So that's out.

Meanwhile, back at the ranch?

Shouldn't Ed McMahon come bursting through the door accompanied by a bevy of beautiful, well-endowed, scantily clad babes with traffic lights for mouths? Shouldn't there be balloons and streamers and banners and a wild brass band and dancing elephants and photographers with cameras snapping my every astonished move? Shouldn't corks be popping out of champagne bottles and raw oysters be slipping enticingly out of shells? Shouldn't someone jump out of a cardboard reinforced vanilla layer cake singing: "You're The Top"? Shouldn't Ed be bellowing above the din: "Congratulations, Victor Stone! You are here! You have made it! You have arrived and the world awaits you!" If not a magic carpet, at least a red carpet unfurled and leading to a snazzy stretch limo complete with soft music, flashing disco lights and wet bar, the ice cubes rattling in the glasses, the Jack Daniels poised. Not this: baggy sweats, unshaved, unshowered, smelling of B.O., cold toast, cooling coffee, an unpeeled banana and no one to share with.

Shit.

The reality being (obviously), you can't plan for something like this. It's like your first sexual experience, or your first roller coaster ride, or dying – you can think about it, you can imagine it, you can devise certain wished-for scenarios, but in the end, it'll happen or it won't, and you'll get off or you won't, or you'll puke or you won't, or you'll dirty your jeans or you won't, and it'll measure up or it won't (or you'll measure up or you won't).

I mean, I must've run through this possibility in my mind a thousand times or more since the novel appeared over a year ago (even admitting it would likely never come about; it was not to be. For *others*, maybe [Elmore Leonard, Annie Proulx, Michael Crichton – already bona fide recognizables], but not me; never for me). Never did I picture this though. At the very least, Kevin shoots on by personally with a bottle of no-name Scotch and we drink it out of plastic glasses. At the very least, I'm shaved and showered and have my clothes on. I've rolled my armpits with Tom's of Maine natural deodorant.

Not this.

Gawd, whine, whine, whine. Give it a break. I've just been told that someone (a complete stranger, no less) is going to pay a million bucks to turn my novel into a movie, no questions asked. Get with the program. There will be time to celebrate later, *turn,*

turn, turn. Right now, do as Kevin says, get dressed, hop a cab, haul ass down to the office and sign on the bottom line. Hell, by the time I'm ready the liquor store will be open. I'll pick up a jug of something to pour into coffee cups. Work tonight? I think not. The environment has sputtered and chugged along on its own for quite some long while and it won't miss me for a night or two. Who knows, maybe Kim can slip out for a few hours; meet me somewhere swank for dinner. If I didn't get the full treatment, she might as well. I'll e-mail her from the office.

Vigilante Editions is located on Spadina Avenue, heart of Chinatown, fourth floor of what once was probably an active, prosperous office and garment manufacturing building, long since vacant and gone into disrepair until someone with more than half a brain got the bright notion to clean up the bathrooms, polish the wood floors, toss on a fresh coat of paint and rent it out wholesale (something better than nothing, right?) to myriad artist types: graphic designers, painters, videographers, photographers, engravers, publishers...folks who would normally be crammed into a basement somewhere or squashed into a den, the walls crawling with 'tools of the trade' and too tight to take a deep breath, never mind light a smoke or pull a cork, without upsetting the whole shooting match. Not necessarily a better class of sweatshop, but at least better dressed, sucking java from a Second Cup travel container instead of a plaid thermos.

It's quite nice, really, and serves the purpose. Outside the large, metal-grid windows, the sight of sickly pigeons, pigeon shit and a further brick wall with its own large, metal-grid windows, sickly pigeons and pigeon shit merely serves to add to the authenticity of the building and reflect its utilitarian function. Perfect, in fact, for the needs, though one has to wonder – for how long? Already, a block south, Queen Street has gotten gentrified with the invasion of City TV, HMV, The Gap and numerous overpriced, overhyped boutiques and beaneries. Adding insult to injury, both McDonalds and Blockbuster have insinuated themselves on the corner, spreading like a virus up two sides of the bustling main artery that is Spadina. Makes you want to plant a few sticks of dynamite and... *BlaMMO!* Blow it up *real* good.

No point, as they'd be back within a month, less than a month, twice the original size and ten times as annoying. Such is the way, grasshopper, of progress, with its fat-cat smile, fat-cat bankroll and displaying little or no taste or concern as to the neighbourhoods encroached upon or the people subsumed. All the strong-willed resolve in the world no match when, all around, the competition withers and dies in the shadows.

You got a problem with that? Huh? You got a problem? Then get the puck out, ya freakin' loser! Make room for the *serious* consumers.

I mean, do I have to be faced with an ad every time I turn around? Subliminal? Hardly. Companies attack openly and full-frontal, from logos on T-shirts and running shoes to giant flashing screens rigged to the sides and tops of buildings. Ads have become an accepted form of violence and violation. Madison Avenue pushing hundredth monkey theory to the hilt knowing that if you say and show something often enough people will not only listen but they'll buy, buy, buy, whether a monogrammed platinum dandruff magnet or a totally disposable Armani knock-off designer travel clothes washing machine – use once and simply toss into the garbage.

And am I the only one who hears the old Campbell's Soup tune in the subway door chime: *ding, dong, ding – mmm, mmm, good*?

Coincidence? I think not.

Playwright Edward Bond wrote: "We can see that most men are spending their lives doing things for which they are not biologically designed. We are not designed for our production lines, housing blocks, even cars; and these things are not designed for us. They are designed, basically, to make profit. And because we do not even need most of the things we waste our lives in producing, we have to be surrounded by commercial propaganda to make us buy them. This life is so unnatural for us that, for straightforward biological reasons, we become tense, nervous and aggressive, and these characteristics are fed back into our young. Tension and aggression are even becoming the markings of our species. Many people's faces are set in patterns of alarm, coldness or threat; and they move jerkily and awkwardly, not with the simplicity of free animals. These expressions are signs of moral disease, but we are taught to admire them. They are used in commercial propaganda and in iconographic pictures of politicians and leaders, even writers; and of course they are taken as signs of good manners in the young. It is for these reasons I say that society is held together by the aggression it creates, and men are not dangerously aggressive but our society is."

"I'm mad as hell and I'm not going to take it any more!" Uplifting sentiment, yes? Well, we all know what happened at the end of that movie, don't we? Our hero gunned down by a member of the audience, the gunner himself a mere cog in a much larger corporate machine running ragtag over the airwaves.

It's true, a few independents hang in there and somehow manage: Cameron House, Artzy Phartzy, The Horseshoe, Steve's Music, Pages Books. Still, no escaping the gnawing feeling in the pit of the stomach, the back of the head, that survival is not merely tentative, it's conditional. Further, it's time-sensitive and the controls are being set from somewhere invisible, unknown, and *out there*.

Or is it me?

Hey – just because I'm paranoid, doesn't mean I'm not being followed!

Anyway, I was in Berlin a few years back, ostensibly

checking out English speaking poetry venues, though mostly there for monkey business as Kim was able to procure a free apartment from vacationing friends, telling them that she was in town for the Canadian Germanic Indie Film Festival where a local flick she'd had some involvement with was to be screened. Involvement meaning she was familiar with the title, *Baal the Jacques* (a title she found particularly pretentious and silly and used [she felt] more to obtain grants or secure a spot in the festival than for any intrinsic value to the work, which, by all accounts, was a pretty hackneyed rendition of a young man's sexual awakening, via the advances of an older man [neither of whom are German and while perhaps having something to do with the god Baal, certainly no relation to the Greek myth or to Bertolt Brecht's play if that was the intention], which ends in bloodshed on the steam bath floor). She'd also had a run-in with the producer *slash* writer *slash* director *slash* lead character *slash* wrists, ha ha, over the phone about receipts.

"I am an artist," he complained. "Not a bookkeeper. The money is spent, that's all you need to know. Where, how and on what is my business."

Right, Jack (or Jacques). I'll just make a note: five grand for coke, stretch limos and bimbos. That should keep the tax guys in Ottawa happy.

Not that she actually said that, though she was sorely tempted, the guy being a first-class jerk and her job at the Toronto Centre For Film, Digital and Video Arts being basically a part-time girl Friday contract where she did everything from stuffing envelopes to ticket sales to assisting with poster design (Fine Arts degree from York University, *BK*: before kids, and handy as she attempts to gain some modicum of independent financial security). In this capacity, she didn't need to put up with either his ego or his tirades: *eet's not my job, man!* Instead, kidded him along, cajoled him into coming up with a page full of documentation that may or may not have been accurate or even real but satisfied the accountants and let them take it from there. For her, water off a duck's ass. No doubt about it, she's smooth.

Anyhoo...a plane ticket and a pass had come available and no one at the Toronto organization was in a position to take advantage, so Kim said, hey, why not, a week out of the country, she *sprechens zie Deutsche* (last name née Wagner and Berlitz school along the way to French, Italian, some Spanish for use in early days of the travel bug and stories of airsick, water sick, parasites, Montezuma's Revenge), our relationship budding and, "Join me in the land of sausage and Nibelung, throw caution to the wind, chance of a lifetime, you only live once, slap it on your charge card, what do you say, lover man?"

What do I say? Twist my rubber arm. Nothing in the works, no star on the rise, been to the Isles once, never on the continent, so far meeting up with Kim as time permits and never overnight, what better way to while away the hours than abroad with a broad getting to know each other crooning a tune in June beneath the moon in the black lagoon (or Black Forest, as the case may be) and liebe, amour, amore (and more and more)...?

We hit the ground running and a quick tour taking the rail from East to West Berlin sketching out the fallen wall and Checkpoint Charlie, the square with a thousand cranes rebuilding, the two of us much more intrigued by the East side with its bombed-out nightlife, entering one old building with a live theatre on the first floor, then ascending in order discovering the doors flung open in every suite featuring a band or guitar player, or art show or performance piece or poetry reading and always a bathtub full of ice and beer being sold by the bottle and a dance club on the fourth floor and another on the tenth that doesn't even get going till two a.m., and gazing out over a balcony spotting a battered airplane strung out in coloured lights, fires smoking in laneways replete with growly, gnarly mutts scratching themselves or leaping for balls, Frisbees, treats, and young folks with green hair and purple hair and tattoos and nose rings and leather leather leather and black pants and black shitkicker boots with beaded inlay and glass and plastic doodads and chains and switchblade knives and Luger pistols for all I knew and music, dancing *mit schnapps und bir, bir, bir...*

Then there was our own sweet tiny apartment with its Juliet balcony, glass doors awash with moonlight that filtered into the room and gave an eerie glow, the two of us dancing tight to jazz on the radio at three in the morning, Billie crooning, Don't explain.

"Are you happy you came?"

"I'm always happy I came."

"Seriously."

"Seriously."

"And you're happy with me?"

"Shall I tell you? Shall I say it?"

She snuggled in closer, kissed my neck.

"No."

We had agreed not to use the 'L' word. Her idea. She wasn't ready. Though the feeling was there and mutual and we both knew it. Still, she said, to name something makes it real and once something is real it has to be dealt with and she had enough reality to deal with at the moment, thank you very much.

Otherwise, we behaved like criminals, creating false identities, plotting schemes, arranging plans to meet up at the various festival events as if by accident: Oh, you're from Toronto. What a coincidence, so am I. Why not join us for drinks, dinner, a free screening of whatever.

Why not, indeed.

Berlin's East side is in stark contrast to the staid West side which resembles any North American city with its clean, happy, moneyed facades and constipated lapdogs.

My advice? Give it a pass. You ain't missing a thing.

Fine, until you realize that the vermin are taking over, that is, East will become West and no use fighting, don't even think about it, it is a *fait accompli,* all in the name of progress; in the name of profits, for, already, Sony and Mercedes are gutting former warehouses and factories in order to transform them into identical New York-style lofts and offices to suit the incoming gentry (architects, lawyers, fashion designers, photographers, glossy magazine editors) and it will be a new-found land of same old, same old replete with fluorescent food courts: Starbucks, KFC, Burger King, Pizza Pizza, Wing Machine, Manchu Wok, accompanied by the obligatory gaudy oversized billboards advertising such local delicacies as McDonald's McSchnitzel und sauerkraut bedevilling the terrain.

Your ad goes here

Meaning, if you're interested, catch it soon, 'cause it won't be long before the soul of the East is sucked out through a plastic straw and shat into the Rhine.

Or am I being overly harsh and pessimistic? Overly cynical? Too much of an old fuddy-duddy? In my book, not by a long shot, and it is simply a matter of dollars and nonsense before Toronto's Chinatown goes the way of the dodo bird and the poor artists who are cached away there are forced to once more relocate to seamier digs.

The oft-repeated story.

But, hey, don't kill me, I'm simply the messenger. Look at

Detroit. Look at Boston. Look at Chicago. Someone's plan to turn downtown into one big nine-to-five office building. Shut down living spaces, move everyone to the suburbs. Raise the rents and get rid of the small fry. Times were good. Cut funds to arts and artists. Who needed them? It was perfect, right?

Right, except no one wanted to come back into town from the burbs at night, so numerous restaurants and clubs suffered or went belly up altogether. Theatres shut down. Tourism flagged.

Right, except that an empty downtown core provided an ideal breeding ground for crime and criminals.

Right, except times got tough all over, so that even the big shots couldn't stay, so vacated the sinking, stinking ship.

What happened? Mayors were eventually elected who realized that downtown should be a beehive of 24/7 activity, a living entity, not a monument to cold cash and stone hearts. The artists were invited back to be a part of the rebuilding; the regenerating, with access to space at reduced rates. After all, what other demographic was not only prepared but eager and willing to live in filthy, broken-down, damp, drab surroundings among rats and cockroaches if only to be part of an active, vibrant community of creative crazies rather than stuck in the burbs with their poisoned green manicured lawns, three- SUV garages and folks made out of ticky-tacky and all look just the same? (Not to make too much of artist types, many as screwed up as the next guy, but, in the main, while often providing society with a good swift kick in the pants when it's needed most, not devising weapons of mass destruction or mailing out envelopes packed with deadly poisons or hacking bodies and storing remains in basement freezers.) Art galleries, opera houses, live theatres were built or rebuilt. Restaurants, bars and grocery stores opened around them and around these grew lofts and apartment blocks and houses. Parks, parkettes and green areas were added (Boston having begun earlier and Detroit still trying to regain its glory days, but the same plan) and the change

44

is telling. In Chicago they spent how many millions or billions of dollars to clean up the waterfront and make Lake Michigan once again safe for swimming. Why? For altruistic reasons? No, for economic reasons. The city was dying, my friend. Dying. The age of concrete and wholesale slaughter and hog bellies was at an end. It had reached its limit and no amount of suave, upbeat, Frank Sinatra tunes (I saw a man, he danced with his wife...in Chicago, Chicago...) could change things. There were too many bodies washing up on the beach; too many skeletons falling out of the closets and nowhere left to toss them.

Do I expect Toronto to learn from the mistakes of other cities? Near as I can fathom, the tendency is yet more mistakes, with the idea that it won't (for some reason I can't seem to grasp) happen here. Reaganomics? Do you have it in the giant economy size? Uncontrolled urban sprawl? I'll take two please. Let business determine what happens to farmland? Well, you kids seem to know what you're doing, why not turn it into a parking lot bathed in buzzy white fluorescent? Gut the arts? Hey, is this the biggest knife you got? Donchya have something with a bit more blade?

Vancouver was the land of plenty, yes? With gorgeous mountains and parks and beaches and never a fear that pollution would raise its ugly head. Today, it's enveloped by a brown smog cloud while rising bacteria levels keep swimmers banned from the water. Much of this due to out of control traffic and out of sight development, the creep of housing up mountains and into farmland serving to destroy the lungs and kidneys of the ecosystem while poor and expensive public transit (never mind peer pressure: what? take the bus? and have people think I don't own a car? I'd rather die) forces the use of the automobile, one nasty business feeding the other like some mad Ourobouros devouring its own tail ad infinitum. Except, we won't last that long at this rate. We talk about the dinosaurs going extinct, ha! They survived for over one hundred forty million years. We've been around a fraction of that and rather than being wiped out by some errant meteorite, we are poised to wipe ourselves out with our own effluent; we will basically drown in our own shit.

In Halifax, the harbour is one vast toxic toilet with nowhere else to flush, so swirls its fume and spume unrelentingly.

And on and on...*yadda, yadda, yadda.*

Gawd, is this what's to become of me? Another cranky crotchety gum-chewing old fart rocking in a rocker on the front porch of an old fart's home mumbling, "Goddamn kids, why when I was their age...," drooling, scratching my balls, wearing a diaper, leaking prune juice from my asshole?

Screw it. Get off the soapbox. I mean, it's not as if anyone listens or cares. It's not as if anything I say can or will make one iota of difference in the grand scheme. Get back to the subject at hand. I'm a millionaire. OK, a half millionaire. Or I'm going to be a half millionaire. Or so far as I know I'm going to be a half millionaire.

Yeah, well, that's positive thinking, isn't it?

I enter the office and everyone has their foreheads pressed into computer screens.

"Hey, whassup, what's happening?"

"Hey, Vic, congrats..." and et cetera.

Well, at least everyone is aware, and for an instant, the world stops and takes notice.

"Vic," says Kevin. "The papers are ready. Just need your John Henry. I'm telling you these guys are primed. Never mind a New York minute, these LA guys are heavy into nanoseconds. Don't they sleep? Is it all cocaine and reds? They've already sent three e-mails: what's happening? What's the hold up? Like I can snap my fingers and you're here, it's done?"

Hardly a breath and back to business.

"I brought us a little something to celebrate," I say, producing a bottle of Jack from a brown paper bag. "Who wants a shot?"

"Bit early for me," says Cheryl, tapping the keyboard. "I'll pass."

"Me too," says Norm. "I've got a rush order to fill."

"Yeah, it'll have to wait," says Kevin. "I've got four books on the go that have to be at the printer's by the end of the week, this being Thursday, meaning I'm at least two days behind where I need to be for a deadline that's at least three weeks past, the worst part being, the books are grunt-work shit."

Not like the old days where an open bottle or a bag of homegrown weed were part and parcel. Today everyone is held responsible and accountable, the priority being to balance the books rather than create them, much of this pressure from governing cultural bodies who appear more and more concerned with their own preservation (meaning, dot the i's cross the t's keep up with whatever is politically correct [or is the new politically correct term for 'politically correct' now 'culturally sensitive'? I'm not sure] of the moment) rather than promoting 'art for art's sake.' A form of control: transform artists into petit bourgeois bureaucrat bookkeeping slaves. Search out the granting formula and fill in the blanks. Which must needs account for the proliferation of so much unadventurous mainstream crap passed off as art. Poetry on the buses and the subways composed and fit to suit the lowest common denominator amassed public, each line stamped indelibly with either a Hallmark card happy face or drippy-dippy glycerine tear, totally accessible, easily consumed and digestible, utterly forgettable and nothing to stick to the ribs or agitate the brain.

On the other hand, one does what one can to stay alive, and unfortunate that the real creative part is often: how manage to satisfy both sides of the equation?

Kevin was having to finance his more alternative fiction and poetry publications by schlepping out trade books, some business/financial, some historical, most quick and dirty unauthorized pop star bios composed of material downloaded from the Net, then paying some poor sack writer to lock him or her self into a room for a week in order to give the mishmash a sort of shape and hip, cool, loose narrative flow. What the world needs, yet another not so in-depth look at yet another not so in-depth teen heartthrob.

Not so hard, the work, really, since most of the books are crammed with photos, the market geared to the eye rather than the brain. Or, more to the point, the genitals, rather than... OK, OK, you get the picture.

"Not even a short one?" I'm ready to break the seal.

"Sorry." Kevin has the contract flipped to the signature page, his name already penned and dated. "Initial here and here. Sign here, here and here."

I sign.

"Anyway, I've got a court date in an hour."

"Yeah? How's that going?" A recent headache for Kevin and the press and one I'm not overly familiar with, as it gets more and more difficult to see Kev without inking in an appointment, though it's a small community and you can't help but pick up things, some accurate, a lot based on conjecture and rumour, most just plain wrong.

"Not bad. Near the end, I hope. The guy's a fucking psycho. We've already shown that the idea for the book came from an old folk tale and he can't claim copyright, but he keeps pulling out these phrases which he says are his, and they're always something ridiculous, like: "The two of them walked down the street." Or: "The one with the red hat." Shit like that that anyone could've written and doesn't prove a thing. Meanwhile, the lawyers get together and argue and the bills add up. On top of that, he sends me threatening letters or phones or e-mails saying he's going to shut me down or ruin me or kill me."

"Kill you?"

"I told you, he's a fucking psycho. Even his own lawyers warn him to stop harassing me, it'll be used against him. Does he listen? No. He says he has connections around the world. One word and, boom! A sniper plugs me through the office window."

"And does he?"

"What?"

"Have this type of connection?"

"He's an ex-officer of a former underground Hungarian intelligence agency that had a reputation for specializing in political assassinations as well as the wholesale elimination of dissidents and other known and/or suspected troublemakers, so, I guess there's a strong chance he might, yeah."

"This is the same guy who writes all those children's books?"

"Istvan Tarnoc, yeah. Fucking psycho."

"How's Allanah taking it?"

"She's a mess. Tarnoc's threatening her too. The worst part is, she's starting to believe maybe she is a plagiarist; maybe she did steal from one of his books. Her mother used to read them to her as a child. I tell her, forget it. She did the same thing Tarnoc did, lifted from a story that's been around for centuries."

"Yeah. Besides, the approach is totally different, right? I mean, hers is a perverse sexual thriller for adults, while his is a short rhyming couplet morality tale for kids. The two aren't even close."

"I know, I know. Doesn't help when someone's threatening to put a bullet in you."

"I guess not. So, what's he want?"

"Whaddyathink? Cash, a public apology, destroy the books already in print."

"Eliminate the letter 'R' from the alphabet."

"Hmm?"

"An old Steve Martin bit, never mind. How did he find her book in the first place? He's in Budapest, right? Allanah isn't exactly on the best-seller list."

"Internet. He likes to check his name everyday to see what turns up. Found a review printed in a University literary magazine that made a one-line comparison between his book and Allanah's. One fucking line and he's on us like shit to a shovel."

"Drag."

"Yeah. Anyway – fuck it. Let's make a date to celebrate. How 'bout Saturday? Paupers at eight?"

I nod. "Can I send Kim an e-mail?"

"She at work? You wanna call her?"

"She's not in till noon today. She might be on e-mail at home."

"Ah."

I had Kevin call her at home once before. The husband answered and Kev said sorry and hung up. The bastard used Star 69 to get the number and call back. Fortunately, Kev was quick on the uptake: Hello, Vigilante Editions. Who? Vigilante Editions. What's that? A publishing house. Uh-huh? Why were you calling here? I'm sorry? Someone just called my house from your number and hung up when I answered. Really? Who would have called there? I have no idea. There are dozens of people working here making calls all the time. It was probably a mistake. Yeah? Yeah. I apologize for the inconvenience. Anything else? I guess not. Thank you. Goodbye. Bye.

Click!

Paranoid, suspicious or what? I mean, who's calling the kettle black here? According to Kim, her husband had been screwing what was commonly called 'the flying squad' for years before she found out and hooked up with me. He worked in the TV industry, occasionally directing (which is what he aspired to and had some talent for) though primarily doing production work (which he disliked but which earned him his daily bread and garnered the full family benefit package). The flying squad referred to that group of employees (mainly young, doe-eyed females) who flitted through the revolving door performing part-time tasks on a contract basis. Not ambitious, up-and-coming starlets looking to fuck their way up the ladder so much as free-and-easy spirits, wanting to be shown a good time. Toss in several late nights working *tête-à-tête* with the manager followed by a plate of oysters, a glass or two of iced Chablis and *honey, honey, honey*. Hell, there was always a vacant director's couch around someplace. If not that, a room at the local Holiday Inn at the preferred customer business rate.

I fire off a quick e-mail. Let her know I'll hang around the office for fifteen minutes or so, otherwise call her at work later and is she able to get away for drinks or dinner or is she on kid duty tonight? I don't go into details 'cause I'd rather tell her the good news personally and figure she'll realize something's up if I'm obviously not going out canvassing tonight.

Kevin shows me the fax confirmation to LA.

"A done deal. Very nice, my friend. Very nice indeed. Saturday we will celebrate. For now, I have a dead horse to flog. Four dead horses."

I sit on the chair by the door, the Jack stashed in the bag, the bag pressed against my thigh. Do I crack it or not? If not, why not? It's ten in the morning. I know if I start drinking now, I'll be in no shape by dinner and is that fair to Kim if she is able to meet me? No. On the other hand, if she's busy, I can get blitzed and it doesn't matter. Should I call the family today or save it? If not Kim, who else can I drag out for a drink? Everyone either married or attached. I could simply drop in on someone, but that doesn't seem to be the way these days, and was it ever?

Remembering back to the so-called salad days, me and a girlfriend dropping in on a guy and his wife and kids on a Saturday or Sunday afternoon, small city of Nanaimo on Vancouver Island. We're over for the weekend to take in the sights, have some fun. He published a number of my poems in a small mag he edited and we'd correspond via acceptance/

rejection letters or postcards and one time he wrote: drop in if you're ever in this neck of the woods. I told the girlfriend this and she said we should phone first and I said why? He said drop in. Why stand on ceremony? Let's do the boho thing and surprise him. She hummed and hawed and eventually agreed. We showed up with a bottle of wine and a bag of nacho chips.

His wife answered the door. She had a kid in her arms and a second one wrapped around her leg. I told her who we were, she called to Richard and shuffled down the hall. Richard appeared and he just looked at me. I hadn't told the girlfriend that Richard and I had never met face to face. Why bore her with small details? Victor? he said. Yeah, I said. And this is... whoever...I can't recall anymore, the brain cells not as bright or as numerous as they once were. Well, come on in. So, we did and we sat around and drank the wine we brought and they had a bottle kicking around and his wife put out some cheese and crackers and sweet gherkin pickles and a jar of salsa to go along with the nachos and it was all very nice overall, though there was some sense of low-grade tension which...

Gloria! That's the name of the girlfriend.

...some sense of low-grade tension, which Gloria and I both picked up on and commented about to ourselves later over fresh boiled snow crab on an isolated beach tossing shells in the sand curling up *nekked* in a blanket with paper cups of best BC plonk red doing the nasty, and which we attributed to our arriving without notice but which turned out to be that we had, in fact, interrupted an argument (and for that, Richard was pleased, or so he related to me in a missive further down the road, also filling me in that the two were no longer together, she had split with the local church minister [praise the lord and pass the ammunition, eh? and what's that all about, playing footsie in the confessional; in the private office: I have had lustful thoughts? Yeah, me too, me too. Oh God, oh God, oh sweet Jesus...]).

Which is, I guess, the point, that you never know what sort

of situation you'll encounter or enter into when dropping in unexpectedly and at least when folks have ample notice or any notice they have time to hide the weapons, stash the bodies and don their best party faces.

Whatever happened to Gloria, I wonder? And that sex-stained blanket? And that '69 Buick Skylark convertible that tooled through the arboreal island landscape spewing ghostly dinosaurs from its rusty tailpipe? Gone. Slipped down the rabbit hole and forever buried, except as memory.

"Curiouser and curiouser," said Alice, feeling very small at the lip.

Eleven eleven – spaghetti time, as my old mother used to say! Kevin's gone, nothing from Kim; Cheryl and Norm clacking away. I'm sitting here feeling like the proverbial lump on the log. What to do, what to do? Go for coffee, read the paper, do the crossword, kill time until I can reach Kim, kill more time until dinner – didn't I once have a life? Has it suddenly stopped? What did I used to do before I became rich and famous? What if Kim can't come out and play? Maybe I should plan to go into work tonight, break the news, take the crew out for a beer? Except I don't have the cash yet and am not sure when I will. What if the producer dies of a heart attack? What if the big one hits LA levelling all and sundry? What if civil war breaks out and Hollywood is taken hostage, brought to its knees, forced to produce only films of high artistic quality, replete with moral merit and a sense of social responsibility and conscience?

Nawww.

Play it by ear, that's the ticket. Relax. Take a walk. Grab a java. Experience Einstein's theory of relativity first-hand as time digs in its heels and drags itself reluctant toward noon.

"Kim?"

"She's not in the office today."

"Not in? You mean, at all?"

"That's right. Can I take a message?"

"No. I'll call her later. Tomorrow."

"She doesn't work Fridays."

"Oh yeah."

"She'll probably phone in for messages if you want to leave a number."

"It's O K. I'm on a pay phone."

"You don't have a cell?"

"No."

"Oh. O K. Well..."

"Thanks."

"No problem."

Click!

A cell? Don't even get me started. I can't stand a land line, never mind be traceable twenty-four hours a day through the ether. What is this twenty-first century need to be connected by voice at all times? Is it absolutely necessary or simply the product of hype? Not so bad if people were having some semblance of a real conversation, if there were some sense of emergency, but most of it is banal and trite and infinitely worse for the rest of us who have to endure it as innocent bystanders over dinner, in movies, at the video store, doing laundry.

Hi, it's me, I'm at Blockbuster. Should I pick up Scary Movie 6 *or* American Pie 4 *or the new Tom Cruise flick that's getting such lousy reviews but can't be that bad if we see Penélope Cruz's tits or the new tearjerker about the idiot savant – oh, that's right, we don't use the term 'idiot' anymore – the gifted mentally challenged whatever guy who sets out to discover the cure for cancer in order to save his ailing wife and at the penultimate moment, seconds before he's able to put the formula on paper, he dies of a brain aneurysm. Meanwhile, the wife goes into remission, and, unable to live without him, kills herself with pills, meanwhile he wasn't actually dead and pops back up in the morgue, the formula having been wiped forever from his brain. Apparently very* Romeo + Juliet, *which I never saw with Leonardo DiCaprio and Claire Danes, so can't say.*

Sometimes I just want to shout: Shut the fuck up! Sometimes I think, tape-record the bastards, then lock them in a soundproof room for hours and force them to listen to themselves on a loop; force them to hear how boring they really are. It's like a goddamn disease. *'Cause, like, y'know, totally, like, the whole, like, y'know, thing, and I said, actually, and she's like, whatever, just totally, flipped, and what's that all about? I mean, like, y'know.* Maybe it should be like smokers, where we need to separate them from the rest of the group, 'cause if you can't get cancer from the cellphones themselves (and the jury is still out on that one), surely you can get it from the steady diet of fatuous drivel that emanates from the contraptions and their users.

OK, I'm not much of a talker anyway as anyone can probably guess, so maybe I just don't get it. Fine, I admit it: I don't get it! The point is, I'm not against talking, per se. What I'm against is talking for talking's sake; talking simply to fill the air with noise, as if folks were afraid of silence. I mean, I have friends (you have friends?), acquaintances, couples, you understand, who talk incessantly. I can only take them in short stints. They have to describe everything they do and repeat it four hundred thousand times (and then there's this use of the word "actually" over and over again, as if it makes some kind of difference to the meaning of a sentence when in fact it is simply redundant. I mean, a thing either is or it isn't; you are either doing something or you're not; the word "actually" doesn't make a thing *more so*. According to the dictionary, the word is "used to emphasize that something someone has said or done is surprising; used when expressing an opinion, typically one that is not expected; used when expressing a contradictory opinion or correcting someone; used to introduce a new topic or add information to a previous statement"), like: I'm taking the garbage out, *actually*. Fine, I'm chopping lettuce for the salad, *actually*. Good, I'll just be a minute, *actually*. OK, *actually*. I'm taking out the garbage, *actually*. I'll chop the lettuce, *actually*. Perfect, *actually*. No time at all, *actually*. The garbage needs taking out, *actually*. You do that, *actually*, I'll do the lettuce, *actually*. Great, *actually*. I'm at the door, *actually*. The garbage, whew!, *actually*. Lettuce almost chopped, *actually*. Back in a shake, *actually*. I'll put in a new garbage bag, *actually*. This one has to go, *actually*. I'm nearly done here, *actually*, the lettuce is almost chopped, *actually*.

It goes on like this. Why? I'm surprised there isn't a call from the backyard on cellphone. Hello! *I'm opening the garbage can, actually.* I'm tossing the lettuce into the bowl, actually. *I've dropped the bag into the can, actually.* The lettuce is in the bowl, actually. *I'm on my way back, actually. The garbage is done, actually.* The lettuce is done, actually...

Cellphone? I'm waiting to invest my dough in a zapper. Something that scatters the frequency within an eight block radius for, say, a thirty or forty minute period. See the reaction. Panic, fer sure. Pandemonium, possibly. Perhaps even riots. I wouldn't be surprised, everyone walking a polite tense edge, needing little to set them off, road rage and finger pointing having achieved epidemic proportions for a nation content to sweep *real* problems under the rug – again, people are starving, fer Chrissakes! Some kid is being knifed for a pair of sneakers! A mother is drowning her children! Somewhere a woman is being stoned to death for accidentally revealing a bit of ankle!

Aaaa, shaddup. Can't ya see I'm on the phone here? Blah, blah, blah...me, me, me... fuckin' screwball freak...

'Course, if they invent the portable zapper, some eager beaver will immediately invent the anti-zapper followed by the anti-anti-zapper followed by the anti-anti-anti-zapper and the war will be on as well as court cases around destruction of property, invasion of privacy, assault on freedom of speech and so on and so forth. Who wins in the end? Who always wins? *Them*, naturally.

That's it then – cut off at the pass.

"See ya," I say, to the office in general.

"Yeah. See ya. Congratulations again."

"Thanks." I wave the paper bag at them. "Later." Cheryl and Norm nod. I figure, sit down to a quick cup of coffee at the Java Joint, catch up on the news, grab a bowl of noodles with won ton and BBQ duck at King's Noodle House, back to the apartment, wait and see if Kim sends an e-mail or gives me a ring.

Since being published by Vigilante I've become a semi-regular at King's, located a few doors north of the office. Kevin liked to frequent the place and we'd meet up sometimes for a bowl. Nothing fancy – big round tables covered in brown paper tablecloths, aged and stained acoustic tile ceiling hung with bare fluorescent lighting, a heater in the corner to warm the winters and a fan for summers, the service minimal, which is fine, as it's fast, efficient and cooks up the best won ton in the city.

Perhaps a tad early for the lunch crowd, I figure, yet the place seems emptier than usual.

"Hey Billy!" I say to the owner, who's wiping down the counter with a dishrag. "What's shaking?"

Billy shrugs. He's somewhere between sixty-five and eighty-five years old, depending on the day, and always manages to somehow keep on top of things.

"Not much," he says. "Business slow. Before, people tell me it's cheaper and quicker to eat down the street at McDonald's, then they say BBQ causes cancer, now they tell me they're afraid my chop suey is gonna give them SARS. Hell, my vegetables come from same place as everyone else's – California, so what's up with that? People just crazy. How's Victor?"

"Good," I say. "Terrific. Some Hollywood producer's decided to put up a million bucks to turn my novel into a movie."

Billy laughs. "That's a good one. You keep dreaming."

"It's true."

"Yeah, sure, sure. You want the usual? Maybe last chance."

"What do you mean?"

"Lease is up and landlord wants to go upscale."

"Upscale?"

"Yeah. He wants to rent to some new cookie-cutter noodle chain. No more BBQ meat hanging in the window, no more handmade won ton, no more ivory chopsticks. Everything canned, packaged and throwaway."

"Noodles R Us," I go.

"The Noodle Depot," laughs Billy.

"Right. So, what are you gonna do?" I'm guessing he's been here all his life and what else does he know?

"Oh, it's not so bad. Who knows, maybe me and my family move to Markham with all the other Chinese. Open a restaurant there. Smorgasbord style, ha ha."

I shake my head and grin.

"No, just kidding. We'll be fine. My daughter is accountant and she invest my money in stocks and apartment buildings that my sons manage. This place more a hobby. And past few years, it cost more than it's worth. So, just as well. Whole world going to rat shit anyway. If people want their soup out of a can, let them have it."

That answers that, I think. Billy taking care of business and not pulling any punches.

"I guess. How long before you vacate?"

"They make me work till end of summer then *boom*, crew come in, do everything over a weekend." He mimes a sort of magical clearing out of the place with his arms. "Been in this spot over thirty-five years; when new people take over, never know I was here." He finishes as if putting on the final touches of paint.

"Well," I say. "I'll see you once or twice before then, I'm sure."

"You bet," he says. "I get millionaires coming in here all the time." He lets out a big laugh, heads to the kitchen and shouts out my order to the cook.

3

Ignotum per ignotius:
The unknown explained by the still more unknown

Snowing like a bastard outside, I enter the apartment, shake off my toque, coat, boots and park them in the closet. I sit at my desk, pick up a pencil, scratch a few lines on a scrap of paper:

> I'm in a blue funk on a grey cloudy day. March
> Bitched right into April with its icy chatter.
> Snowy and cold? Jee-zus! It's still cold.
> Hey, have you got the sniffles?
> Do you still eat rosehips?
> Do you still do that thing you used to do
>   with the warm brandy rubbed into your nipples?
> Or was that for something else?
> Seriously, can the weather affect a person's mind?

I've decided to use more weather imagery in my work. My thinking is, no one talks about poetry while everyone talks about the weather. Maybe I can reach a few more folks through the back door. Unlikely, but at least displaying a sense of humour amidst the usual doom and gloom existential angst. Three messages blinking on the answering machine. I hit the button.

"Hi, it's me, Maja. I was thinking about you recently and thought I'd call to see how you were doing."

This is my ex-wife, formerly named Susan. Formerly being before she saw "the light" and found "the way." Direct upon the heels of our wedding, she decided she wanted to explore her spiritual side. Was it something I said? Something I did? Or merely her way of immersing herself in an enterprise that was specifically for her, given the fact that I was a confirmed atheist (recollecting Gore Vidal who said whenever he felt the urge to believe in God he read the headlines in the morning paper, which instantly quelled the notion)? And why wait to drop the bomb until after the vows were made? Not that I'm intolerant, simply that, coupled as we were in close quarters, there was more than a fifty-fifty chance we'd eventually rub each other the wrong way. Which is, in fact, what occurred.

Anyway, after checking out the various possibilities, she did as many lost sheep do these days who are unwilling to accept any of the already existing total package deals: she did a mix-and-match, created a belief system that suited her – the best of the East meets the best of the West plus whatever else in-between outer space New Age pseudo-science voodoo mumbo-jumbo inner child magic that caught her attention, from Jesus to Buddha to Jung's archetypicals to First Nation totemics to ancient guardians to circle formations to the entrails of chickens (or the entrails of carrots in her case as she also turned vegetarian around the same time): so long as the teachings were all round and soft and fuzzy, meaning that anything that smelled of base or bottom line or hard and fast rules or commandments *to-be-adhered-to-come-hell-or-high-water-or-else-suffer-the-earthly-punishment* or eternal damnation by fire or bowing and scraping to a (especially) patriarchal figurehead had its butt kicked unceremoniously out the door, *feng shui very much*. And sex? Let's not even go there, literally. "My body is a temple" sort of thing.

Part and parcel with this new philosophy came the obligatory name change and why is it these folks always need their moniker to end with a vowel, I wonder? The softness, I suppose, the openness, though to my bent mind, seems it's to keep them ever-prepared to suck God's dick – *ahhhh!* Which is the one consolation I could take from it all, that my competition was the Big Guy, so, in the end, no contest, hence, no failure.

"I had a dream the other night," she continues.

She does this a couple of times a year, calls me up to see how I'm doing. Sometimes she hits me with a "dream" or a "vision" or a "feeling" (believing she is able to dialogue with spirit guides and such, she has set herself up as a combination healer, seer, geomancer) that she needs to express. These usually take an oracular form and thus can be interpreted in a dozen different and assorted ways (to me, you understand, not to her, who manages to identify solid clear messages in soap bubbles, cloud formations, tea stains and so on). *I see two roads (or two doors, or two rivers, or two anything). You will have to make a decision.* Well, no shit Sherlock! Can you be a little more specific? *No, but you will know when it happens.* Is there a time frame I should be looking at? *Soon.* Uh-huh. "Soon" for me who believes that death is the great equalizer or "soon" for you who believes in life eternal? We go on like this and always end with her laughing, saying, *Take it for what it's worth. I just wanted to share it with you.* Nice of her, really, and sort of fun, though lacking the drama of: *You vill meet a tall dark stranger vith a scar shaped like a crescent moon on hees left cheek. Bevare thees man, for though he promeeses reeches he brings only ruin. The next several months are imperative. Be on your guard at all times.*

You betcha.

"In the dream you were standing in the middle of a bridge, as if you were unsure which way to go. There was a plaque at your feet that read *Deus ex machina*. I also sensed a name – *Lucian* or *Luciano*, it wasn't quite clear. Do you know anyone with that name? He or she will have an effect on your life. Anyway, hope you're well. Call me if you want. Bye."

The name already having an effect on my life as I attempt to figure and/or configure. *Lucian*? *Luciano*? I'm drawing a blank. What about *Deus ex machina*, eh? Fairly common phrase. A god from a machine, used in reference to forced or unlikely events introduced in a drama or novel to resolve a difficult or awkward situation, derived from the use of deities in the ancient drama. Certainly not foreign to Susan – I mean Maja (still not used to it) – who is, at bottom, an intelligent woman as well as a practicing family lawyer with Bennett, Boggs & Fox. "Stuck in the middle of a bridge." OK, another decision-making metaphor, so no big deal. Don't know anyone named *Lucian* or *Luciano*, I'm almost sure, though the trick here (always) is that background becomes foreground as soon as something is highlighted and suddenly the name jumps out from every weird direction. As well, could just as easily turn out to be Lucia or Lucy or Larry or a dog named Lucky or a boy named Sue, for that matter. In truth, I don't know what counts anymore, as the slippery slope seemed to get slipperier and slipperier when Susan (rats, Maja) and I were together.

So: Lazarus, Lorenzo, Lupino...then Martina, Nicholai, Oswald, Penelope, Quentin, Roderick, Sylvester, Tom, *Victor*, and so on through the alphabet.

I can see this is going nowhere, so, move on MacDuff!

Second message is male and begins with laughter: "Ha ha! Hi! You don't know me. I called the first time by mistake, hung up, then decided to hit redial so I could listen to your message again. It's hilarious. I even told a friend to call and she said the same thing. Hope you don't mind."

Maybe that was Lucian? Maybe the friend was Luciano? Plus how many others that he's contacted and given my number to? Lena, Lorna, Lanny, Louis, Louella, Louise. All hanging at the end of the connection. Or *dis*-connection, in this case. Can a phone line be considered a bridge? Feeling stuck in the middle *fer sure* and God undoubtedly in the machine since how otherwise explain a mess of wires translating electric pulses into human language?

Message three: "Hi, it's Kim. I need to talk to you."

Always ominous, those words. Like: "We have to talk" or "There's something I have to say or tell you." Could mean anything, though usually bad news from my own experience. Maja (good!) sitting me down once or twice a year, more often as things declined, with me eventually playing the heavy and initiating the discussion: we don't talk, you don't appreciate me, I need your support, we don't agree on anything anymore, you ignore me, you don't understand me, I've changed, you've changed, we have nothing in common, what are we doing/ where are we going? and the entire litany of clichés that are not clichés when they centre around yourself. Or *are* clichés but no getting away from or skirting around, they are that stubborn and ingrained.

"I'm not even sure about what," Kim's voice continues. "I'm a bit stressed right now: work, kids, Michael and I behaving like I don't know what and excuse me for sounding maudlin but tension so thick and obviously present you can cut with a dull knife and mainly trying to avoid each other which I know doesn't help but easier in the day-to-day. Difficult when living under the same roof, sharing the same bed (though not sharing, *that way*, you know, at least, not so much any more, the motions, is all, really, me not interested, him the same, I think, but, the motions, the facade, you understand, not the same as with you, I mean...I mean...I'm sorry, this not coming out right, forget it, it doesn't matter [I mean, it matters, but...] never mind, I'm just...

ohhhh, whatever) and the dog sick and another two hundred bucks for a vet and medication and Michael not wanting a dog in the first place, and me (but you know this already) thinking that the girls should have a dog at their age, before they get too old. I'm rambling, I'm sorry, like I say: stress. Though maybe period coming on. Breasts tender, though may have been from you the other day, giving them a workout. Not complaining, it was divine. Still...need to come to some sort of...of...I don't know. Maybe. I'm on kid duty tonight. Aren't you going into work? Are you sick? Is it the weather? How is tomorrow for you? Afternoon. Kids will be in school, Michael working. I'll call first. Where are you? Sorry about this message. We'll talk."

I don't know why she apologizes, this being a pretty typical communiqué from her and a close match for the way she talks in general, moving topic to topic and difficult to nail down, especially in terms of answering a question. Even something as simple as, What are you doing this afternoon? will solicit a circuitous response with a mind and direction of its own that will encompass everything from soup to nuts to fashion to politics to music to what's planned over the next month – everything – excluding the answer to the original question. It's a trait which I both love and abhor, depending.

Meanwhile, what's to be made of this latest dog's breakfast? Better to not even go there. Pick out the positive parts (tender breasts from previous lovemaking) and leave the rest. After all, by tomorrow (or by later today, even) she may be in an entirely different frame of mind and most of what she mentioned here will have been forgotten. Besides, it's been about eight months since she last broke off our relationship (a record, I think, over the nearly three years we've been seeing each other) and I don't want to upset my day by contemplating another sad session involving reasons why we shouldn't/can't be together: security, house, history with husband including mutual friends and family, guilt, fear of unknown and better the devil you know than the devil you don't, fear of looking like a bad person, fear her children's psyches will be utterly destroyed and they'll grow up to be druggies, alcoholics, suicides, axe murderers, bankers, Alliance Party members, and will hate her for betraying them and so on, guilt and fear as well around the feeling I'll get bored with her and drop her or find someone else or maybe later screw around or leave her for someone younger, sexier, more attractive, more interesting, more, more...*whatever.* Legitimate concerns on some level connected to lack of confidence undercut by the fact that she no longer loves her husband, is no longer excited by him, doesn't want to lead a double life, loves me, is excited by me, realizes her kids must know or sense something is not right and how does that affect them now and in the future? Easier to sever relations with me. Short-term at least, whether a few days or a few weeks, broken by a casual meeting or a tense phone call and need you, want you, sorry, sorry, and back between the sheets. I mean, clothes simply have no chance remaining on when we get together. Buttons and zippers positively *pop* and *zip*. Natural materials become foreign and synthetics virtually peel from flesh. I'm not bragging here. I am merely saying *what it is* about the two of us together.

Oh yeah, other things in common as well.

As swell.

OK. As I can't remember what I taped, I hit the message record button to hear what the guy found so goddamn funny.

"Hi, I'm Vic's toaster. The answering machine went bust and I'm filling in. The other appliances are jealous. Tough luck for them if Vic likes me better. I make perfect toast every time. Well, nearly every time. The thing is, I'm not sure exactly what to do, so please make it short, sweet and to the point. I don't want Vic to have to pry the message out of me with a knife like the time the bagel got stuck and, well, it's a long, sad story, so, never mind. Wait for the beep."

Funny enough I guess, especially since most folks now use a

service and all you hear is, "You have reached *blank*. Leave your name and number after the beep." Not too creative or personal but it gets the job done, I suppose.

So, no Kim until Friday, which is a drag. Do I call Maja back? No. At least wait and see if anything happens. Or maybe call her back with a story? Concoct something. Take her for a ride. I could name the LA movie producer Lucian. Or tell her I've met a certain special *someone* – Luciano – tall, well-built, attractive, sexy, who has stolen my heart and shown me what it's like to love another man. Uh-uh. Truth is, for a writer, I'm lousy at make-believe when it comes to situating the circumstances in the real world. Maybe not enough control. Besides, I'm happy to keep a certain amount of distance between me and Maja, and to call her with the news of my good fortune might come across as sheer gloating.

Which leaves me right back in limbo. I check the time and it's two forty-five. Out the window huge snowflakes are wheeling through the air and piling against cars and sides of buildings. I can hear the wind rip. Maybe I should take a trip to Mexico. Sit in the sun. Ogle pretty señoritas. Drink tequila and *mucho cerveza*.

Right. Money burning a hole in my pocket and I don't even have it yet. What I need is some sort of adventure to occur. Something to keep me occupied. At least until tomorrow afternoon when I can share the news with Kim. Forget Lucian and Luciano. A call from a total stranger. A knock on the door. Perhaps a woman selling encyclopedias:

Mick heard a knock. He wasn't expecting anyone but he also wasn't especially in the mood to be alone. What the hell, he figured. Answer it. See who's who and what's what. Maybe a little excitement. Maybe nothing. He grabbed his tumbler of bourbon, sauntered across his ramshackle apartment and swung open the door. Standing in front of him was a dame.

But what a dame. She was young, blonde and built for action. A honey. A real knockout. Hi, she said. My name's Candi and I'm selling encyclopedias. But, I don't think it's a set of *books* you need today. With that, she threw back her shoulders and thrust out her chest. Her breasts were large and full. Beneath her flimsy white blouse, and slung as they were in their elastic harness, they resembled a pair of torpedoes ready for launching. Oh yeah? said Mick. You don't think I could use a little more educating? Oh, I think you know your way around the block just fine, she said. Well, replied Mick. I know a hawk from a handsaw, a bible from a bowling ball. And I still know how to slice the melon, if that's what you're into. Sure, she said. I'm not big on charades but I've never been one to pass on a game of *she sells sea shells*, so, why are we wasting our time out here in the hall talking? Mick stepped aside and allowed her to enter. Come and take the load off your feet, he said. He tried to help her with her sample case but she just grinned, picked it up like it was a bag of marshmallows and sashayed her lovely derrière across the beat carpet. Which way is the war room? she teased. There was nothing else for the two of them to do. Their eyes were burning holes in each other's clothing. Just follow the tread marks, darling, said Mick, who pointed the way and followed her to the bed.

Yeah, the terrific stuff of cheap paperback novels, whereas what really happens is:

There was a knock at the door. Tom wasn't expecting anyone but he also wasn't especially in the mood to be alone. He shuffled across the carpet in his slippers and got a static electricity shock as he grabbed the handle and turned it. Ah, jumped Tom, as the door swung open. A woman stood there. She was rather skinny with mousy brown hair, thick glasses, thin lips and bad complexion. She wore a brown camel hair suit that buttoned up to her chin. There was no sign of breasts beneath the drab material. Hello, she said. How are you this fine day? Absolutely tip-top, said Tom. And yourself? Extremely fine. Thank you for asking. Not at all, said Tom. I see by your sample case that you are a seller of encyclopedias. You might well judge that I am, indeed, a seller of encyclopedias, yet I prefer to think of myself as a purveyor of knowledge, set out on a quest to satiate a populace starved for mental sustenance and stimulation. My name is Wilomena Goodchild – not my *given* name but my *chosen* name. I am a healthy and energetic twenty years old. I am currently enrolled at the university where I am studying a broad array of subjects in a variety of disciplines, from anthropology to Zen, from mathematics to metaphysics, from Sappho to de Sade. Pollution, revolution, constitution, absolution and ablution. I am a vegetarian. I neither drink nor smoke. I have never taken a drug of any kind either legal or illegal. I am pure of heart, sound of mind and hale of body. I have three complete and satisfactory bowel movements a day plus a colonic treatment once a month, which is considered the norm for maintaining a germ-free system. I plan to have my B.A. at age twenty-two, my M.A. at age twenty-four, my Ph.D. at age twenty-seven. Naturally, by this very age of twenty-seven I will also have amassed a comfortable fortune through hard work and sound financial planning while at the same time having provided people of all race, age and colour with the means and tools to achieve their own inner peace, happiness and material wealth. I will accept all of this with my usual modesty, which will raise me in good stead with both friends and those established in positions of power. I will marry a loving, caring, famous artist and will bear two wonderful, smiling children. A boy and a girl. As you may now well perceive, this, and more, can all be yours as well, for there is absolutely no reason I can imagine why you shouldn't purchase a set of encyclopedias and begin to establish your own highway toward a piece of heaven on earth.

Oh my god, oh my god, oh my god. Is this too fucking unbelievable or what? Or strictly fallout from my past relationship? Am I a magnet for this type of woman? Are they attracted to me in the same way cats like to sit on laps of people who are either afraid of, allergic to, or don't like cats? Do I do something about it? See a shrink or an exorcist? Though Kim appears safe enough. Just the other problem of being attracted to a woman who's married with kids. Been there before and where did it get me? Shunted off for the same old reasons: fear, security, comfort.

Stop snowing *fer Chrissakes!*

Now I'm trying to change the weather, as if this were easier. And who knows, perhaps it is, human relationships being a sort of Gordian knot rife with twists and turns, laced with shards of glass and packed full with deadly spiders. What is it they say? A conundrum wrapped up in a paradox stuck inside an enigma?

Yeah, then shoved up your arras, har!

It's too much. I pull the bourbon out of the bag, take my only real cut-crystal glass off the shelf and pour myself three fingers. I mosey up to the window and face the storm. *Cheers,* I go. *To me.* The phone rings.

"Vic?" says the voice.

"Yeah."

"It's Ray."

"Ray! I was gonna call. Tell you I'm not comin' in tonight."

"That's OK. We've cancelled the canvass because of the weather."

"Oh, right. It's really comin' down."

"Yeah. There's something else. Thought you might've already heard, maybe got a call, but I guess not, eh?"

"Heard what?"

"About Eileen. She died."

"Died? What are you talking about? I worked with her last night. She was fine. She joined a few of us for a beer after the shift. How could she die?"

"Brain tumour, apparently. At least, that's what I heard. Nothing official. Seems she collapsed on the street this morning, they took her to the hospital and that's where she died. She had Peter's phone number in her pocket, police called him and he called me."

"Wow. So, what else? I mean, is there going to be a service or anything?"

"Not sure. You know what she was like. Maybe just wanted cremation and flush her ashes down the toilet. Hope someone on Bay Street chokes on them."

"Yeah. Well, keep me in touch. Let me know what's what."

"Yeah. OK."

Didn't seem like the right time to tell Ray my news. Eileen, I think. Dead. Of a brain tumour? Made sense, in a weird way. She was one of those types who, according to her, had it made from the beginning – upper-middle-class family, father a doctor or a lawyer, mother also a professional of some sort, though can't remember what, exactly. Eileen able to go to university and study whatever she wanted, so merely dabbled for years. Finally decided to pursue a career as an artist and started up her own company doing faux finishes and such in private houses and offices. Very successful. A woman with a lot of talent, drive and ambition. Then one day, someone – a relative, an uncle, I think – came down with some mysterious disease or other and Eileen chucked everything to take care of him. Eventually, the man died.

This is where things get funny. Strange funny. She believed that his death was neither an innocent illness nor an accident; that there was a combined private sector and government conspiracy in place meant to kill her uncle then hush things up. It had something to do with experiments that he was involved with and included toxic chemicals and illegal dumping and the pollution of vast areas, which he wasn't involved with directly but suspected was occurring and believed was causing sickness, birth defects, death and further nastiness among the local populace.

Again, things are fuzzy from my side, having really only picked up bits and pieces from Eileen over time (I had been on the job a relatively short period, maybe a year and a half, with her bopping in and out of the city for various reasons, showing up to canvass when she needed cash, occasionally meeting afterward in the pub over beer, plus her being the type to more often rant or lecture rather than converse which caused me to shut down or fade out or ignore in the main, so...). Besides, the entire premise sounding very hokey, very movie-like, very *Erin Brockovich* complete with a boob enhanced Julia Roberts, thus very suspect, though the thrust of the story being, I gather, that the man was possibly a whistle-blower or going to become a whistle-blower or had come across as a potential whistle-blower and Eileen figures they (the conspirators) shot him full of poisons and wrote it off as a hazard of the job, the man not taking proper precautions and so on and so forth. She tried to go after the culprits (or who she perceived as the culprits) but couldn't prove anything so it went nowhere. Since then (this being several years now, I'm unsure as to how many, but a fair chunk of Eileen's adult life, guessing, say, ten to fifteen), she's thrown herself into being an environmental activist as a way of trying to bring about something positive from the man's death.

In the meantime, she also felt that whoever was responsible for his death now had it in for her as well; they were watching her and it was simply a matter of time before they made an attempt to eliminate her in one way or another, so she had to remain constantly on guard.

To my mind, Eileen always came across as a bit unhinged and whether because of the experience around her relative's situation or aside from it, it was always difficult to take her seriously. Part of this is, I suppose, because I'm not into either zealots or conspiracy theories as a rule and everything for Eileen revolved around her miss know-it-all, holier-than-thou attitude and her belief in one conspiracy theory or another, such as, The world is controlled by three major corporations with their offices buried deep underground in the deserts of New Mexico, one of which is Coca-Cola; all elections are fixed and tyrants are placed in power in order to make democracy appear more desirable than it really is; AIDS was created in a laboratory in Antarctica by a special interest group of wealthy neo-Nazis as a means to destroy blacks and gays; most so-called natural disasters are in reality man-made and the weather is being altered in order to control the production, availability and cost of crops and livestock.

You get the picture.

As well, there appeared to be a lot of internal, personal anger for who knows what reason or reasons, which frequently turned to rage over nothing in particular. Case in point: her early marriage. You don't even want to go there. I tried and I can only guess at what happened and none of it appeared good: drugs, alcohol, abuse of all sorts, abortion; threats of murder, threats of suicide from both parties involved. The venom would fly from her mouth, then Eileen would clam up tight. "But that's over now," she'd say. "That's in the dark past."

Right.

Or her sister who works as a CPA for some multinational insurance company. Or doctors who want to drug her with antidepressants and sleeping pills. Or her parents who she says turned their backs on her and her uncle. Or her berating me one night with her hypothesis that my own personal bugaboo was fear of success, arguing that there were several instances when my world became severely disjointed precisely when things were getting comfortable both personally and financially. I mean, c'mon, give me a break! Fear of success? That's crazy. And yet? Anyway, it was like sitting next to a time bomb. You knew it was ticking, but you never knew when it was going to go off. Who knows, maybe the brain tumour had been sitting there like a sharp-nailed finger for years scratching away at the grey matter and this was the real cause of her fixations. Again, the ghost in the machine working its nasty black magic.

I throw myself on the couch and turn on the radio. A woman sings a jazzy version of *On the Sunny Side of the Street*.

"Huh." I stare out at the blowing snow and picture Eileen as the tortured shape in Munch's *The Scream*, shivering on a street corner selling wilted roses. "It figures." I raise my glass. "To Eileen," I say. "Wherever you are."

4

Spero nos familiares mansuros: I hope we'll still be friends.

Drag myself naked out of bed, stumble to the bathroom, collapse onto the toilet, do my little thing, exalt in the pleasure of a good morning dump which also serves to remind me that humankind has not progressed very far from its apelike ancestors. You'd think by now we'd have evolved some other type of system, our assholes sewn shut, the urethra knotted, waste material somehow turned to rose water and simply evaporating through our pores into the atmosphere. While we're at it, why not sex via the Vulcan mind-meld and the delivery of babies given back to the stork? Yes, the entire gamut of bodily functions made sanitary and pleasant, almost sacred.

Why not? I'll tell you why not. To begin, the folks on Wall Street and Madison Avenue would have a fit. What to do with themselves without peddling deodorant, toilet paper, disposable diapers, condoms, mouthwash and Preparation H? They'd be on this notion like shit to a shovel (as Kevin is so fond of saying), visions of expensive condos, fully loaded SUVs and fifty-two-inch flat screen TVs flushing down the drain, throwing tantrums and screaming bloody blue murder claiming that their livelihood was being taken away and how could this be permitted?

Like, this has never happened to a group of people in recent history: that the rug has been pulled out from under due to some sort of technological innovation or change, right?

Wrong!

Secondly, perhaps more importantly, certainly more naturally, it's a well-known fact that the horse and the lizard are still battling it out in the old brainpan with neither appearing about to back down or give in, so the likelihood of any of us evolving much past the Australopithecus stage is pretty remote, meaning, we are biologically constructed and hard-wired to continue, for the most part, with these behaviours: eat, sleep, shit and fuck. Add to this fact an article I once read by some I-can't-for-the-life-of-me-remember-the-name psychologist who stated (I'm paraphrasing) that, in terms of human consciousness, we haven't moved much beyond the Pleistocene epoch, it places us in a rather dark and dismal light indeed, making it difficult if not impossible to blame the suits for everything wrong and miserable in the world whereas the suits are simply in step with their basic natures and born to thrash it out among the rest of the bulls and bears.

One simply sometimes wishes that *occasionally*...

As for me, I'm not beyond enjoying the pleasures of the flesh, though fully aware that the brain is the most erotic organ of the body and in need of similar exercise and stimulation. Though difficult at the moment with the blood pounding in my temples and the voice of Johnny Cash kicking up gravel with his boots. "Woke up Sunday morning with no way to hold my head that didn't hurt. And the beer I had for breakfast wasn't bad, so I had one more for dessert..." Nothing nowhere near the truth, naturally, it being Friday morning, no beer in the place and Johnny a mere sense memory come back to haunt.

Toss my naked rack into the shower, pop a couple of Tylenol and feeling much better *thankyouverymuch!* Maybe almost able to face the day and reacquaint with the problem at hand, that being: what to do, what to do? beyond reconstructing the events of last night, which are obvious and straightforward, as highly evidenced by the detritus strewn about the kitchen: bottle of bourbon two-thirds vanished, crystal tumbler in the sink alongside dirty plate, dirty knife; alongside empty sardine tin; alongside empty cheddar cheese wrapper; alongside eggshells; while on counter, tipped opened box of Triscuits, dill pickle bottle and I'm thinking at least I had the wherewithal to eat, otherwise who knows what worse shape I'd be in? Best thing to do is clean up the mess, the hour drawing almost near enough to "phone home, ET, phone home" and break the news of my good fortune not-so-gently to the family, while also expecting a call myself from Kim and whatever it is that's on her mind (and hoping it's neither too serious nor too involved as I'm a party waiting to happen and what's wrong with this picture? alone again, again alone, just me and the dishes and *this* close to a half million dollars and wanting to spread the joy and wealth, baby!).

The phone rings on the other side of the country and my brother answers.

"Hey, Stu, what's up? It's me, Vic!"

"Big brother! How's it goin', bud?" Stu's attention splits between me and one of the kids in the background. "Settle down. Can't you see Daddy's on the phone? Sorry about that, Vic. I got the three of them home this morning. Brian should be at school but he's down with something. What are you down with, pal? He's not talking. Bit of a fever, couldn't keep breakfast in his tum-tum. Isn't that right, sport? Probably just sick of school. I'd've sent him in, to tell the truth, but you can't these days. They send 'em back just as quick. Kid has a sniffle or sneezes and right away it's the plague. What the hell, with all the time off kids get these days, what's it matter? Surprised they learn anything. Not like when we were in school, right? Melissa, watch your brother. Melissa's usually pretty good with the boys but she woke up on the wrong side of the bed too, so it's whine, whine, whine. Yeah, you can watch TV soon. I said *soon*. I'll tell you when. It's like this all the time. We gotta put a limit on the TV otherwise they'd watch it twenty-five hours a day, eight days a week. So, what's on your mind? Why'd you call?"

"Well, you know..."

"Sure, sure. Must be nice, the single life; no kids. Not that I'm complaining, I love my kids, it's just that, some days – Melissa, what did I say? Here, take your brother for a sec, Daddy's arm is getting sore. I think I've been carrying Bobby in the same arm since he woke up. It's cramping. Melissa, don't give me that look. You know I don't like that look. She has this look, y'know, like someone's driving spikes through her eyeballs and all I asked her – don't you start to cry now. Like I say, some days... Otherwise, being the house husband is pretty good. I get to watch my kids grow. Unless I kill them first, ha ha. She's crying. OK Bobby, upsadaisy. Try the other arm. Em went into the office early. Big deal going down. Don't ask me what. Finances. She wants to be the breadwinner, that's great. Makes sense that I stay home and...not yet! What did I tell you? What did I tell you? That's right. 'Cause who's the boss? Yeah, OK, Mommy's the boss. You're right. Smart aleck kid. But I'm the boss while Mommy's away. Sorry Vic, you caught me at a bad time. Not that there's ever a good time anymore. So...?"

"Yeah, that's OK. Listen, I just wanted to tell you some good news. You know that novel I wrote? Stu? I sent you a copy."

"Sorry Vic, I wasn't listening. Brian was heading down the stairs. Had to catch him. How did parents ever manage without the cordless phone, eh?"

"Yeah. I don't know. Anyway, the novel I wrote last year..."

"Right. The novel. I didn't have a chance to finish it. It was kind of weird."

"Yeah, anyway, some Hollywood producer has decided to turn it into a movie and I'm going to get half a million bucks."

"Uh-oh."

"What?"

"I think Bobby just dirtied his drawers here. Man, what have you been eating?"

"Did you hear what I said?"

"Yeah, that's a good one, Vic. Very funny. While you're at it, pull the other leg."

"It's true."

"Sure it is. Whatever. Listen, Vic, I'd like to talk and I know you're pissed off 'cause things are so crazy on this end, I'm sorry, but, maybe another time, y'know, when Em's around and I have, like, two minutes to myself."

"I'm not pissed off."

"Right, right. Doesn't matter. I gotta change a diaper. That's my life. And you know what? I like it. I like my boring life. You wanna play the big star living in Toronto, that's fine. Right now, I can't talk. I'm sorry. That's the way it is, OK?"

"OK. Another time."

"Yeah. Anytime. Only, not now. So long, Vic. Good talking to you. Really. I'm sorry you're pissed off. What can I say?"

"It's OK. I'm not pissed off."

"Holy crap, Bobby! You won't believe this, Vic, it's like— fluorescent. What the hell goes on?"

"So long, Stu. I'll be talking to you."

"Sure. S'long, Vic."

That didn't go quite as smoothly as I had planned. Then again, it never does. And why should it? Say what you will about each of us having the power to direct our lives, things suddenly shift when separate individuals come into contact and their agendas fail to match up. It's a wonder any of us are able to talk together at all except around the safest and most mundane topics – jobs, weather, dirty diapers and so on. Anything beyond that and it's like everyone's orbiting separate planets and speaking separate languages. I dial my Mom.

Ring, ring, ring and maybe she's out already. Retired for years and managing to be busier now than when she was working, between helping out at the Seniors' Centre, raising money for the local hospital, playing golf, line dancing, taking night school courses in ceramics, Chinese cooking, photography and who-knows-what-else?

"Yes?"

"Hi Mom. It's me."

"Victor?"

"Uh-huh."

"Well, this is a surprise. Is everything all right? I've been watching the weather channel and it says there's a blizzard in Toronto. And blackouts. The traffic's not moving. Everyone's stuck indoors. Are you stuck indoors? They show shots of different areas and it looks dreadful. It's hard to tell if that's where you live or not. You really should send along a photograph sometime so I'd have a better idea."

"Yeah, well, you know, the media exaggerate and things always look worse through the camera. There's snow falling, but it's pretty normal for this time of the year. Most of the time they're talking about north of the 401. Downtown is never that bad."

"They mentioned blackouts downtown specifically."

"Maybe. Off and on. I haven't had a blackout." I take a peek at the VCR to see if the clock is flashing, just to be sure. It's not.

"What about SARS? I understand two more people died. It seems like every time I turn on the news there are more deaths. Are you taking precautions? Are you washing your hands? Do you think it's safe going door-to-door these days? You never know what it is you might be exposed to. You're not going to

Chinatown are you? Apparently they now think that the virus is transmitted by animals. My God, it's getting so you can't do anything these days without worrying what it is that might kill you."

"Yeah, I know. But seriously, SARS isn't the epidemic people are making it out to be. It's pretty much contained and the people who are dying usually have other health problems to begin with."

"That's what they tell you. I also read that there's been a lot of covering up, and not just in China but in Toronto as well. I'm sure there's more going on then they'd have you believe."

"You're probably right about that, Mom. Meantime, I don't know anyone with SARS. And not many people are walking around wearing face masks. A lot of folks jump every time someone sneezes or blows their nose, especially on the subway, but, again, I believe it's the media making the situation out to be far more horrific than it really is. It's their job, y'know. The worse the news, the more people listen. Human nature."

"Still, better safe than sorry and I'd feel better if you were living here with your friends and family rather than being alone in Toronto. Besides, it's a well known fact that people move from Toronto to Vancouver to live and not vice versa. I have friends that tried and they said they'd never go back to Toronto even to visit."

This is a subject Mom never gets tired of – me moving back to Vancouver – even though I'm forty-five years old and I've lived here almost ten years now and insist that I'm happy in Toronto. The problem is, the reasons I give for staying don't fit her world view. If I were still married with a job, kids, a car and a mortgage, she'd understand. It would make sense. She still wouldn't be completely happy, but it would make sense. To say that I enjoy the energy, that I feel more at home among the people, that I like downtown as opposed to the suburbs, that there are more things that interest me in terms of art and culture (especially the literary and theatre scene), that I have a better shot at having my work published – *"And what's the big deal about having your work published if it doesn't pay you any money?"* Right. – streets full of ripe mangoes when the weather gets hot (speaking of weather, wasn't it Somerset Maugham who said, "A writer should experience life in the summer and write about it in the winter," which makes Toronto and its long winters pretty much perfect), able to order 'cold tea' in Chinese restaurants past the liquor law hour and be served beer disguised in stainless steel pots, is too nebulous and transient. It's not family. As I realize there's no point in turning over the same old tired ground, I attempt to change the subject.

"Along those lines, I have some good news."

"You're moving back home?"

"No."

"Then, what do mean, 'along those lines'?"

"I mean, I have some good news."

"Yes, but I was talking about you moving back home and you said 'along those lines,' so I expected..."

"What I meant was, 'along those lines' in terms of me being safe and happy."

"I don't understand. How can you be safe and happy when you're living in a city with eight months of wintry blizzards and blackouts and SARS, then unbearable sticky heat waves in the summer and more blackouts and West Nile Disease and pollution and skin cancer and no real job."

She has a point, though I really don't want to go there. Just lead to further endless spinning of wheels, gravel flying discussion going nowhere and I need to move on, in more ways than one.

"What I called to tell you, what I want to say is..." Mom continues her litany of examples. I wait until I can get a word in and feel she's listening. She takes a breath and I jump. "I've been offered half a million dollars by a Hollywood producer to have my novel turned into a film."

She barely breaks stride.

"What do you mean, you've been 'offered'? Is someone giving you half a million dollars or not?"

"Yes."

"Do you have it?"

"I just signed the contract yesterday."

"And it's sure?"

"I signed the contract."

"A contract doesn't mean anything these days. I read that there are certain producers who make all sorts of wild offers never intending to honour them."

I often wonder precisely where my mother gets her information and why she chooses to believe certain aspects (the downsides, usually) rather than others. Case in point: what about the producers who *do* honour their contracts? Or does the media consciously choose not to print this information? Or are people so jaded or so programmed that they are only tuned in to pick up on the more seedy, tragic side of the news?

"It's being handled by my publisher which means it's being handled by his lawyer, which means..."

"Lawyers aren't to be trusted so much either, these days, from what I gather. You get a lawyer involved and you'll be lucky to see five cents of your money."

"Yeah, maybe. But, at some point, you've got to trust somebody."

"You can only trust your family. Everyone else is out to take advantage. Your problem is, you're too trusting. I can't say you didn't come by it honestly. I was the same for years. Your father taught me better."

Another topic I didn't want to get sucked into – the downfall of my parents' marriage and the eventual bad split.

"All I'm saying is, my publisher has checked it out and everything seems in good order. I mean, he's getting half a million as well, so it's worth it for him to…"

"What do you mean, he's getting half a million as well? Why? He didn't write the novel. You wrote it."

"It's in the contract we have. The publisher gets half of what he sells to TV, movies, foreign rights, whatever."

"And you signed a contract like that?"

"It's standard."

"How do you know it's standard?"

"He told me."

"Your publisher told you?"

"Yeah."

"And you believed him? Did you look into it yourself?"

"Mom. C'mon, he's also a buddy."

"Uh-huh. So much the worse for that."

"What do you mean?"

"All I can say is that friends have been known to slit the throats of other friends while they're sleeping for considerably less amounts of money."

"I guess." There's a slight disconnect over the phone.

"I've got someone on the other line. It's probably Jenny calling about what time to pick me up. Jenny's very nice but has a terrible sense of direction. I have to explain in detail how to get here every time. I hope I didn't sound too negative. It's great news, if it happens. Because you can never be sure. Don't count your chickens before they're hatched. But if it does. You'll be able to afford to come back home to Vancouver. Be with your family. Get yourself set up in something. A job. Maybe meet someone. That would be nice. I'll call you later. Bye. I love you."

"Love you too. Bye."

That leaves my sister Leigh, who (fortunately) will be already hard at work, plying her trade as a seller of hot tubs. Hard to believe a person can make a living (never mind a rather decent living) selling hot tubs in a city that doesn't see that much sun in a year, but, there you go. Shows what can be done when everyone gets together to push a certain location as Canada's west coast paradise, God's country, la-la land – where a half-hour drive ('cause no one wants to take public transit: in the first place too crappy, in the second place too uncool) can bring you to the beach, the mountains, the country and a bit further will even take you to the desert or rainforest. Milk flows from fire hydrants, fruit hangs ripe for the picking from street lamps, animals practically shed their skins and toss themselves on BBQs, there's a Starbucks (or two) on every downtown street corner, marijuana has been more or less officially declared the city flower and folks get lit up hassle free anywhere, any time, anyhow.

Simply forget about the traffic, the crack cocaine, the poverty, the pretentiousness (what's that joke? When a guy from Toronto says, "Go fuck yourself!" it means "Have a nice day," and when a guy from Vancouver says, "Have a nice day," it means "Go fuck yourself!"), the creep of houses up the mountain and down into the farmland, the skyrocketing costs of everything. Lie back and do the Timothy Leary thing, man: drop out, tune in, turn on – Ommmmmm. I mean, it worked for San Fran, right? And aren't we become a rather (albeit fuzzy, yet...) close reflection of our southern neighbours, what with us importing and devouring their books, their TV programs, their movies, their music, their food, their clothes, even identifying with their tragedies way more than our own – a question: if twin towers fall in Canada, does it make a sound? If it does, does anyone hear? Does anyone care?

I have the distinct feeling I'm repeating myself and it's true that sometimes I do go on and on like the proverbial broken record, but, until someone listens and circumstances change, there is little else to do and I am merely siding with Franz Kafka when he states that "It is perhaps well to write down warnings frequently."

More about my sister. She's married to a great guy named

Gord who is in the construction business and whom she met and got to know while the two haggled over the purchase price of a personal hot tub resulting in an invitation to come over and test out the installed product. They have two great kids, a boy and a girl, a great dog, a great cat, a great house in Burnaby with a great two-car garage to contain their two great vehicles – a minivan and an SUV – a great hot tub, a great neighbourhood with great neighbours. You get the gist. Things are great for her. This is the life she chose, she's happy with it and I'm happy for her.

When I say it's 'fortunate' that she'll be at work, it means I don't have to call her right away. After the previous two family conversation fiascos, I don't think I could take another, as I've got a pretty good notion of what would ensue. I mean, when it comes to two separate individuals speaking two separate languages and orbiting two separate planets, we pretty much fit the bill and hard to believe that we were spawned by the same parents and raised in the same household. In fact, we are about as polar opposite in our thinking and behaviour as two people can be, and, how does that work? It's like Heraclitus versus Plato: the flow versus the fixed. For me, everything exists in shades of grey. The universe is constantly in flux and subject to change and a stone today might turn out to be a bird tomorrow. For her, everything is either black or white and what was true yesterday also holds true today, tomorrow and the day after. Mine is the world of shape-shifters and middle grounds, hers is the world of absolute forms and a clear idea of 'the Good.' And when it comes to art (especially mine), her opinion is that it is at least three steps removed from 'the Good' and falling further away by the moment.

To add fuel to the fire, she deep down feels that my brother and I have pissed most of our lives away due to too much drinking, womanizing and just plain fucking the dog rather than settle down and carve out a niche for ourselves in the world.

A man has it made, she'd say. *Just mess around until some female comes along who's stupid enough or desperate enough to welcome him inside her house and take care of him before he packs up and leaves because he's decided he's bored or finds some new woman who is as equally stupid or desperate as the last one.* Ouch. Harsh.

What's that joke? What do you call a guitar player without a girlfriend? Homeless. I told this to my sister once. Didn't crack a smile, just looked at me, like: whatever.

More content with my brother now that he's married with children (though still with her eyebrows raised around the househusband bit – *if he had a real career that paid real money they could afford to hire a nanny*). Unhappy with me in that she knew Susan (Maja) and got along with her and thought she was "good" for me and how can I be so intolerant as to leave her simply because she found God? Telling me I should be so lucky to find something to believe in. Without getting into the nitty-gritty details, I told her she really didn't know how deeply Susan (Maja) had thrown herself into the God business nor how much it affected every aspect of her (and mine as a consequence) life. She said it didn't matter. Marriage was a sacred bond till death do us part. I could only bow my head and sigh. Fine.

Imagine what the response was when I told her I was involved with a married woman. I was home for a visit around Christmas two years ago and I approached her as she was pouring a glass of white wine for herself in the kitchen. I was cautious and waited until she finished pouring and the glass was secure in her hand. She pretended to take it calmly but there was a definite black cloud forming above those dark raised eyebrows and flashes of lightning escaping from back of her eyes.

When she hears the news of my good fortune her reaction will be something along this line: It figures. It's just like you, the way you live your life, the way it's always been for you – fall into a shithole and come up smelling like a rose. Meanwhile, the rest of us slave away at our jobs and earn our money honestly by the sweat of our brows (and so on...). Unwilling or perhaps unable to concede that to write a book takes a great deal of time and effort and is, in the end, work. Or as likely going on at length that half a million dollars isn't that much these days and not as if you can live off it forever, especially with interest rates being so low and no head for investing and no real job to fall back on when I piss the money away ('cause that's what I'll invariably do, *piss it all away,* she knows this for a fact, what else would I do?) and perhaps repeat to me (with obvious relish) the story of the ant and the grasshopper, ha ha.

"...the lazy grasshopper stuck outside shivering in the cold of winter, freezing his ass off, while inside the industrious ant is lounging in front of a warm fire sipping brandy and eating chocolates..."

OK, I'm exaggerating slightly. At bottom, of course, my sister loves me and I love her and we want the best for each other. Even her comments (which can appear so injurious) I accept as coming from a place of truly heartfelt caring and a desire to help. Again, simply the result of two separate individuals with two separate languages orbiting two separate planets having to communicate together on some meaningful level and it is damned difficult if not downright impossible for any given length of time. But, we try. We try.

Though not today. Not with Leigh at any rate. She's at work and I am off the hook for an indefinite period. Besides, Mom will likely broach the subject and Leigh will have rationalized it by the time I talk to her and she will have her happy face on and the waters will run smooth as silk.

The phone rings and it's Kim. She wants to meet at the Second Cup in the Annex around two. I ask, why not come here? She says no, the Second Cup. She hangs up. This is not a good sign. This is the old: *I'll give him the bad news in a busy restaurant so there won't be a scene and I can slip out quietly when it's over*. Not that this has ever happened to me personally or to anyone I know, so far as I can recall. It's something I'm only familiar with from TV and the movies, where the ploy invariably fails, yes? Besides, I'm not the type who creates scenes and she knows it. No, the real reason for meeting in a neutral location is that she's afraid that if we are alone in my apartment her resolve will melt and we'll end up between the sheets.

Then again, maybe I'm being overly suspicious; maybe I'm totally off track here and she has something else to discuss and time is an issue; maybe...

Maybe, though unlikely. I watch the clock creep toward noon.

The storm has eased since yesterday. I live on Bloor at Shaw, southeast corner and, as the Annex is close by, I figure I'll get some fresh air into my lungs by doing the fifteen minute walk. It'll also allow time to think. About Kim, mostly, and previous breakups. Usually over the phone, sometimes by letter, either sent through the mail or slipped under the door, a couple of times got together at my apartment for a drink, then the talk, the tears, the one last time in the sack, another occurrence *out of the blue* in a quiet corner of a pub. Normally her idea to split, though mine at least twice, and always around reasons of security (or insecurity), the kids, the relationship being stuck and it not being enough for either of us to be strictly an affair and where do we go from here?

Speaking of separate orbits, how does it happen that two separate satellites come into contact and begin to enter into a relationship in the first place? The idea that Kim and I met one night as I canvassed her neighbourhood conjures interesting possibilities, mostly of the pornographic kind. Urban tales of hot horny housewives opening their doors and their legs to all sorts of plumbers in need of unplugging, electricians in need of rewiring, cable guys in need of rechannelling, priests in need of defrocking and so on. Save the environment? Oh yes, I'm totally interested. Absolutely. Come inside, you must be damp and cold given the weather, sit down, relax, have a drink, tell me more, I love the way you say "wildlife," it sounds so rugged I can almost hear the growl, my goodness is it getting hot in here, or what? Why don't you climb out of those wet things and slip into something more comfortable, like, fer instance, *me*.

Nothing of the sort happened, of course, either with Kim or with anyone else. Not to me, at any rate. A guy I worked with, though, had a story. His name was Barry and he was one of the few men (OK, the only man) I had ever met who was an honest-to-God babe magnet. He was young, good-looking, well-built, smooth-talking, personality to burn, from a moneyed family, did all the rich folk sports: golf, tennis, squash, racquetball, waterskiing, snowboarding, downhill racing, horseback riding, scuba diving.

Sitting in the bar, women would turn and stare, mesmerized; they couldn't turn their eyes away; they'd glide by the table to get a better look; they'd raise a bit of skirt to show their legs or do the bunny dip to flash some cleavage; they'd write their phone numbers inside matchbook covers and fold them into his hand; they'd dump girlfriends and cheat on boyfriends and Barry would accept it all with total modesty and a smile. *Yeah*, he'd say, *it's always been like this with me. I don't know what it is. Really, while most men have problems meeting women, my problem is getting rid of them.*

What it is, is that all satellites have not been created equal and a rare few are somehow able to suck lesser satellites toward them with either little or no effort.

Out canvassing, he learned quickly that it was easier to push for bigger donations from a few houses than squeeze out small donations from many houses. Especially in the suburbs where lawns were advertisements for pesticides, and recycling bins were used to store a glut of children's toys, Barry admitted to going in with total attitude, vowing not to budge from the doorstep until the occupant paid for at least a year's membership in Friends of the Ecology. Even if he had to shame them into it. Which he sometimes did, and delighted in, to hear him tell it. Though more often than not he'd play them at the status level: *Listen, I'm just like you, I earn my money, I pay my taxes, my parents have a cottage in Muskoka, and I agree it's the government's job to do something about the environment. But, come on, you know and I know that the government needs to be pushed if you want to see any real action. And who's going to do it? Are you going to do it? You don't have time for that, right? But, for a mere twenty-five bucks a year, you can have Friends of the Ecology do it for you. I mean, maybe there is no real garbage problem and maybe there is no such a thing as global warming. Maybe it's all the ravings of a bunch of crazed tree huggers. Then again, maybe not. You have children. Why take the chance? You want to give more, I'll write you a tax receipt. You can't lose. By the way, I notice you've got the skis packed. How's the powder? Over Christmas I was doing downhill in Colorado. That was sweet.*

And so on.

He'd make his quota *plus* in an hour and a half, then go sit in a local bar or coffee shop and work on his screenplay until he had to meet up with the rest of us battered souls in the van, sharing war stories about how heartless the bastards were and how we'd come away empty-handed. Amazing.

Anyway, we were in Rosedale one night and a nanny answered the door. Apparently she was a knockout, which I believe. Barry began his spiel in the usual way and she just stood there shaking her head. Turned out she could only speak a few words of English. He figured she was Russian or something – tall, blonde, buxom. He decided to alter his approach and his objective. Fuck the "saving the environment" game, let's play the "try to score with the nanny" game. He went with the "me Tarzan, you Jane" routine, using monosyllables and simple hand gestures, writing down his name and number: *Me Barry. Barry. Yes, my name. Barry. Your name, what? Tasha? Good. This my telephone. My telephone. You understand? No, forget earlier. Forget it. No ask for money. No money. You, me, go out. Go out, yes? A date. You phone me. I take you out.* Him turning the fingers of one hand into walking legs to illustrate the two of them going out.

Impossible? She called the next day, the two went out, he banged her and that was the end of that. Would he see her again? No way. As with everything else that he was involved with, the thrill was in the sheer novelty and once the objective had been accomplished, it was on to the next conquest. Meanwhile, the women would keep phoning, keep dropping into the bar, their orbits so close yet so far apart, and no chance in hell of ever re-entering the sphere since, for Barry, these women had ceased to exist. There was barely any memory they had ever existed except as maybe minor blips on the radar screen. He hadn't merely shifted universes, he had slipped through a black hole and travelled into a whole other dimension of space and time.

Meanwhile, back at the ranch.

Kim and I collided at a party following the preview of a local feature film. An actor buddy of mine had a small part in the flick and was able to invite a few people. It maybe doesn't have the same flair as being seduced in suburbia, but there were definite theatrics involved and heavy leanings toward the erotic. I saw her standing at the bar and immediately thought, ohmygod, she's gorgeous. Who is she, is she single and if she is, how do I get introduced? I was fresh out of marriage (the legal part, that is, the rest having done a couple-of-years slow dissolve, the both of us realizing things were getting worse, not better) and, while undoubtedly horny and on the lookout, I knew there was something more going on with respect to the presence of this particular woman, beyond the fact of her being gorgeous. There were only a few times in my life when I was instantly infatuated with someone and each of those times led to long-term relations. In other words, I'm a firm believer in love at first sight. I shuffled over to the bar, insinuated myself beside her and immediately gave a sidelong glance at her wedding finger. There it was, all right, in all its symbolic glory, that perfect circle of gold topped with a floret of sparkling diamonds. Shit.

I turned to the bartender. The booze was free and I asked for a scotch.

"You can order single malts."

The voice came from her.

"Sorry?" I said.

"You can order single malts, if you'd prefer. It's a full bar," she said.

To be honest, I don't like most single malts. Except for the peaty ones, and at that moment I couldn't for the life of me remember a name.

"Johnny Walker will be fine," I said.

"Red or Black?" asked the bartender.

I looked at Kim. "Surprise me," I said, which I thought was pretty damn clever considering I had no idea what to say next. She seemed to be opening the door toward some kind of conversation, I just didn't know how to step in.

Fortunately, Kim had no problem in that department and the next thing I knew it was: What did you think of the film? Simple, yes? A no-brainer. Trippingly off the tongue. I sent the ball back. Oh, not bad, though the story was kind of flat. Yeah, she said, I thought so too. And clichéd. Right, I said. And the direction was sort of all over the place. And that lead actor? Ha ha. The both of us laughing as we basically trashed the film on every level. Then her talking about being somewhat in the industry though really her husband and onto the kids and what do I do and me giving the quick and dirty about having finished an M.A. and a bit of this and a bit of that and a book of poems and more about her family and her husband not being here tonight, taking care of the kids and I'm thinking, well, gorgeous, yes, and nice to talk to and have a drink with and might as well enjoy 'cause that's all there's going to be, her obviously happy and better not to even think about trying anything even remotely covert or underhanded.

Except, it turned out that she had spotted me earlier and had positioned herself at the bar in such a way as to get a closer look and was astonished and excited by the seeming coincidence that I had chosen this spot at the bar to order my drink and she knew she had to talk to me and she was already aware that there was something in the wind and that the two of us...

She was maybe getting ahead of herself, she thought. Though as it turned out she wasn't, and so, the entire theory of coincidence gone flying out the window with the realization that we were fated from the start and no avoiding our orbits drifting ultimately together and interlocking.

Of course, we didn't know this yet. We walked (staggered) to the subway and said good night. Under the pretense of maybe being able to recommend me for some sort of nebulous writing job she asked for my phone number. A few days later she called. We had coffee. We set up a date for lunch. We discussed reasons for my marriage breakup and her own marital woes. I invited her over to my place for a drink. She hardly got through the door before we jumped each other. We never made it to the bed. I had the presence of mind for only two things. Number one, a condom fumbled from my wallet. Number two, at the penultimate moment, after I had brought her to orgasm with my finger, and learning she had never had sex outside the marriage, I leaned back and said: OK. I just want you to know that we can stop right now if you want. You can go home and not feel too guilty. You can tell yourself you fooled around a bit but never went all the way. She just stared at me wild eyed and naked and said: Are you joking? With that, she grabbed my ass and drove me inside her.

Like I say, definitely theatrical, and heavy leanings toward the erotic.

Kim is sitting at a corner table in the back. We're still at that awkward, uncomfortable stage where we have to be careful about who sees us together, under what circumstances and how often, though my friends are aware and several of her closer friends and only a matter of time before the shit hits the fan. Meanwhile, behave as if we're pals in public even as we have hands misbehaving behind backs and beneath tables. I mean, seriously, who in their right minds couldn't tell, couldn't know? And yet, partners are always the last, right? And much to do with shared history, expectations and a certain amount of trust built up; lines drawn in the sand: you can go this far and no further. Except the lines move or get pushed or fade or disappear altogether, depending. Otherwise, disinterest and a grown lack of caring, I suppose: he does what he wants, she does what she wants, so long as the machinery keeps moving and no one loses sight of the status quo. There are, after all, the children to think of, the in-laws, the weekends with friends, the mortgages, the trips to the cottage, the holidays in Spain, the latest sporty SUV with surround sound stereo and built-in DVD player, the pet budgie, the dog, the gerbil.

I grab a coffee and join her.

"Hi there," I say.

"Hi," she says, and I sit and she begins with an apology for dragging me out on a day like this then into a quick rundown of what's happening at work and at home and the kids and what's up with me, though not waiting for an answer, why wasn't I at work last night, was I sick, am I sick, and about the damn dog again, though a good dog and worth it but why now, to the vet, and medicine so costly and the dog spitting out the pills and proper technique, her demonstrating, difficult holding the dog's jaws open with one hand, trying to fire the pills down the throat deep enough with the other, and I nod and go, oh yeah, uh-huh, and she doesn't have a lot of time 'cause something's come up at work and she has to meet a friend to help her move a dresser and kids home from school and groceries to pick up and her husband pissed off about cutbacks and where will the axe fall next the whole industry shaky at the moment and why is there always a million things to do and no time to do them and me trying to be somewhat calming by simply listening to her 'cause I am familiar with this scenario and her way of talking herself out though that uneasy feeling that she's building up to something else and eventually, yes, she does get there.

"Vic," she says. "I know I've done this to you before and I hate to do it, because I do care for you. I do. But I'm afraid and I've been thinking about this and I know it wouldn't be fair to the kids and it would kill my parents and upset our friends and I don't have a real job and if I did how could I be with my kids and how could I support them otherwise and it isn't fair to keep you hanging on and it isn't fair to Michael 'cause I told him when I found out that he was fooling around that I wanted to make it work, though he's not really interested in me *in that way,* not really, though he says he is. Anyway, you've heard this all before and I'm sure you're bored and up to here with it anyway. I mean, it's best. It really is." She slides my apartment key across the table. "I'm sorry."

"Listen," I say, and place my hand on hers. "I've got some good news, great news even, that might make things easier and help change your mind."

She shakes her head and stares down at my hand.

"My novel is going to be turned into a movie. Some producer in Hollywood is paying me half a million bucks for the rights. I'll be getting the money any day now."

"Are you kidding?"

"No. I swear. Kevin called me yesterday. I went in and signed the contract. Look, I love you, I'm saying it, I want to be with you and with all this dough, plus the fact that my book will sell more copies, you don't have to worry about the financial part."

Kim takes a second to think. "That's great, Vic. It really is. I'm happy for you. I am. And it's sweet of you to offer and to say those things. The thing is...there's more to it. I can't bring myself to put the kids through a divorce. I don't want to be blamed for ruining their lives."

"But you'll feel OK ruining your life?"

"It's different with me. I'll manage. Besides, it's not about me, it's about the kids."

I consider challenging her statement using arguments from basic psychology: you don't do your kids any favours by living a lie and ruining your own life, they'll only hate you later when they find out, things won't get better only worse, your real fear is that you'll be seen as the bad guy so it is about you. But we've been there already on numerous occasions, so a waste of breath.

"Kids adapt. The money means you don't have to worry about getting a job. You'll be able to be there for them; help them through."

"No. In fact, the money makes it worse."

"What are you talking about? I thought you were worried about security?"

"Yeah, but don't you see – if I say yes now, people would believe I was doing it for the money."

"You're nuts."

"No. I'm not. Even I might believe I was doing it for the money. As an easy out."

"I don't believe this. Before you couldn't do it 'cause there was no financial security and now you can't do it because there is. That doesn't make sense."

"I'm sorry. All I know is that if I were to leave Michael, it would have to be in my own time and be my own decision based on where I was at. I have to feel secure in myself that it's the right decision for everyone."

"That's your biggest problem. You want to please everyone, make everyone happy, and it can't be done in most cases. It certainly can't be done here. Someone has to get hurt. You're hurt, I'm hurt and in the long run, your kids will be hurt."

"I'm not so sure about the kids being hurt. As for you, you'll be all right. There's always been plenty of other women just waiting for me to be out of the picture."

"Mostly in your imagination."

"But not totally."

"I only saw other women when we went through breakups, never when we were together. And not every time then, either."

"And those women are still around. I see the way they look at you. And now that you'll have money, it'll only make it worse. You'll have to beat them off with a stick."

"I love you. I want to be with you. Is that so hard to understand and accept?"

"Until some young honey comes along and you begin to compare. I can't match up. I'm not twenty-one anymore. I've had two kids."

"You're beautiful."

"That's nice of you to say. Do you get to go to Hollywood and meet the cast, go to the parties?"

"Yeah, I guess. They might fly me down to sit in with the screenwriters. They don't want me to say anything, just watch. I don't know about parties."

"Right. It's the movie business. There's always parties and always young women throwing themselves around. I've got to go."

"Kim...?"

"No, really. I've got to. Congratulations, Vic."

She grabs her stuff, gives me a quick kiss on the lips and swoops out of the place. What the hell goes on here? This is not the way things are supposed to happen. My universe becomes darker and less populated by the second.

Home again, home again, jiggedy-jig. Visions of *Blade Runner* in my head and for what reason? Four messages blinking on the telephone and I punch the button.

"Hi, Vic. It's Ray. Thought I'd fill you in on the latest about Eileen. Basically, she was cremated and her ashes have been sent to her parents in Florida. She had it all set up ahead of time with a friend. No funeral, no service, nothing. I'm inviting the canvass crew to the office tomorrow afternoon, Saturday, from three to six. Very informal. To pay respects. There'll be beer, wine, snacks. Hope you can make it by."

Bim, bam, boom. Like that. Which doesn't surprise me, knowing Eileen, except I had almost imagined: the discovery of a box full of papers and other evidence surrounding the chemical conspiracy, a stack of incriminating tape recordings, or at least a note fingering the possible culprits should she one day mysteriously disappear or suddenly die.

Message two is my sister.

"Hi, big brother. Mom called to tell me the news. Congratulations. That's great. I guess now that you're going to be rich and famous you'll never talk to us again. Just remember, though, half a million dollars doesn't go that far these days, so don't go pissing it away. You've got your nieces and nephews to think about. Which reminds me, do you have a will? Of course you don't. Well, get one, otherwise it's the family that's left to straighten out the mess. Oh, Mom says you're considering moving back to Vancouver? I told her more likely LA, which really choked her. Gotta go. Bye."

That was two strange calls together. Eileen dead and buried and me quick on the heels. A will? These are become serious times all of a sudden. What happened to living in the present and *la vita loca*?

"Hi. You don't know me." A woman's voice. "A friend of

mine gave me your number and told me to call to hear your answering machine message. I was afraid you might be home, but luckily, you weren't. I'm glad I called. It's very funny."

How many friends does this guy have? How many have called and not left a message? Lucky is right. It'd be terrible if you had to talk to me personally as I'm not that funny live. Wait a minute. Lucky? Lucky Luciano...

"Vic. It's Kevin. Listen, something's come up and I can't meet you tomorrow night after all. The good news is that the money has arrived from LA I told you, these guys don't sleep. I think it's all orange juice, coffee and reds. Come into the office Monday around noon and I'll give you a cheque. We'll do lunch. You can treat, ha ha. Also, get your bags packed. You're going to California. They want you at the studio Wednesday to meet and talk promo. There'll be a ticket for you at the airport. Do these guys work fast or what? I think the script's written and they want the movie out in the fall. There was some mention of Ben Affleck and JLo, if you can believe it. See ya."

Ain't that a kick in the head. Believe it? At this point, I'll believe just about anything. Though the present burning question is: what do I do tonight? Must be someone free to go out for dinner or a few drinks or shoot some pool. Who do I know that isn't otherwise married or involved? I dial my actor buddy, Karl.

Karl, I say, what's up? Crazy busy, he says. He's on his cell. I'm on my way to an audition. Oh yeah, for what? Who gives a shit? It's a commercial. I think it's for a bank. Karl is the same actor friend who said that TV would slot an entire program of two dogs fucking if it would sell an extra bag of potato chips. He's also the one who invited me to the preview where I met Kim. Karl canvassed for a while, then quit to go back to catering. Said waiting on people was less degrading than begging for money, even if it was for a good cause. What are you doing tonight? I've got the kids for the weekend. I'm making them dinner, then I head out to do a function for a bunch of rich, right-wing assholes in Forest Hill. last time I was there, our respected Premier was a guest. He showed up drunk and continued to get drunker. At some point early in the evening, he goes into the kitchen and starts grabbing the ass of every young woman there. They had to hustle him out the back door before anyone caught him. Promised the women there'd be "a little something extra" in their pay envelope. Right. More likely told them they could keep their jobs if they kept their mouths shut. *Noblesse oblige*, I say. Yeah, says Karl. What's that line by Dorothy Parker, I say? One drink I'm under the table, two drinks I'm under the host? Ha ha, right. Except the host was already taking it up the ass from some real estate developer, ha ha. Yeah, safer to go after the hired help. I gotta run. How 'bout if I call you next week? We'll get together. Sure, I say. Early in the week. You got it, buddy. Ciao, he says. Ciao, I say.

I dial Robert, a poet friend.

Robert, I say. It's Vic. How's it goin'? OK. You? he says. Pretty good. Can't complain, I say. Yeah, no one listens if you do, anyway, right? Robert laughs. Right, I say. Are you busy tonight? You wanna maybe go out and have a few drinks, shoot some pool or whatever? Um, can't tonight, says Robert. I've got a date. A date? Anyone I know? Don't think so, he says. I met her a couple of weeks ago at the Rex. Well, good for you, I say. How 'bout going out now for a couple of drinks? We could meet at the Victory. No, I'm filling out a grant proposal. Has to be in by Monday and I'm barely started. You need to be a freaking Philadelphia lawyer to figure these things out. Don't they know we're supposed to be artists, not goddamn bureaucrats or accountants? Yeah, I say. I don't tell him I found the form rather straightforward and sent mine in a week ago. It's more procrastination and bullheadedness on Robert's part and perhaps a desire to dis the system. Funny thing is, Robert has received this grant twice in the past while I've never had a sniff.

A moot point, considering what's recently occurred. Besides, he says, I don't want to be shit-faced when I show up for my date, if you get my drift. Got it, I say. I'll let you go. Be talking to ya. Yeah, he says. Later.

I flip through my address book. That's it. That's my so-called circle of single friends. There's no one else. And Robert has a date, so who knows if or how long before he enters that further circle of friends and acquaintances who are locked in with partners and/or kids – which is the way it is when you reach a certain age and no family of your own. I check the Festival guide for a decent movie at the reps, preferring them over the cookie-cutter theatres with their lineups, their lousy overpriced popcorn and garish lobbies. There isn't. I glance at the bottle of bourbon.

"Looks like it's you and me again," I say.

I pour a shot and take a sip. Maybe I'll head back to the Annex; have dinner at the Victory. It's become a real hangout for artist types. Who knows, maybe I'll bump into someone. Maybe I'll meet someone new; maybe hook up with a fascinating stranger – *Lucinda* – who'll "have an effect on my life." Yeah, like maybe take me back to her place and fuck my brains out.

Naw.

Besides, I hate going out and eating dinner alone. What sadder picture is that? Most likely grab Mexican takeout from up the street, stay home, watch TV and whack off to *Red Shoe Diaries*.

God, I'm boring.

The office gathering's pretty subdued. Going on three-thirty and, out of the fourteen or so canvassers on payroll, there's about half of us here. I suspect the atmosphere will change somewhat as more folks show and a bigger dent is made in the booze.

It's an eclectic crew with everyone except Ray being strictly part-time and focussed on other endeavours, meaning, a few are students working on degrees at U of T, several are trying to make it as artists, musicians, writers and so on while some are simply lost souls or social outcasts with no other type of work that's suitable for them. I'm somewhere in the middle. While most of us care about the ecology to a certain level, none are what you would call career environmentalists. Eileen is about the closest. *Was.* Of course, there are also those who are there strictly for the paycheque. Barry is one of these, not around today as he generally heads home on weekends. Most, though, have an honest interest and go out in the field hoping to make a difference. Personally, I wouldn't want nor would I be able to sell something I didn't believe in. This isn't altruism, it's simply the way I'm built. I mean, I'm no salesman in the first place and just manage to squeak by out there. If I had to bullshit my way through, I'd likely burst a blood vessel. That old saying: "You're so full of shit your eyes are brown." That'd be me.

Simon shuffles over. He's a gay, black dude with long, spindly arms and legs and a goofy smile. He makes puppets and masks and puts on shows for kids. Usually in the parks during the summer. He is (or was, I guess) probably Eileen's best pal among us and they'd meet for coffee outside work and she'd help paint the miniature sets he'd construct.

"Vic! Glad you could make it." He gives me a hug.

"Hey," I shrug. "Wouldn't miss it. Sorry about Eileen. It's weird, eh? How are you taking it?"

"Oh, you know." He steps back with his arms spread and bobs with his knees and head in such a way as to suggest springs in his joints. "She was a troubled soul and not really meant for this world."

Simon seemed to travel in and out of a sort of New Age spiritual realm depending on his mood. One day he'd speak in terms of *the* God, the next day it would be *a* god or merely *the gods*, the next day it might be Gaia or the Great Spirit or the universal consciousness or the collective unconscious or, "that whose centre is everywhere and whose circumference is nowhere," and the day after that, annoyed at someone, saying: Don't be a damned fool! There is no God. God is an empty noise. Someone said that. Someone famous, though I can't remember who.

"You're probably right," I say. "She seemed to carry a lot of demons inside her." I edge toward the drinks table. I'm a trifle hungover from the night before having, in fact, managed to drag my sorry butt out of the apartment and into the Annex where I sat at the bar in the Victory eating a dirty burger and polishing off a bottle of house Merlot. Old habits are hard to kick and I still couldn't get myself to order a nice, expensive Masi or Beaujolais. Not strictly for my own benefit, at any rate. Now, if Kim had been with me...different story.

I pick up the jug of Chilean red and fill a plastic glass.

A few more of the crew arrive even as others leave, so there are never more than seven or eight of us at a time. I speak with Shelley about her English class. She's saved Shakespeare to the end of her B.A. because she feared him and was hating every boring minute of it. I say I had done the same thing years before for similar reasons, but was fortunate to have a prof – a Jewish woman born in the Bronx – with a great sense of humour and a background in Freudian analysis. The woman rolled up her sleeves and invited us to do the same, grabbing hold of each text firmly by the genitalia and not letting go until we had satisfied every iambic moan and groan. Turned out to be one of the best courses I ever took. Lucky you, she says. My prof handles everything with kid gloves, treats every text as sacred and coats it with a particularly repugnant air of ingratiating solemnity. It's disgusting.

As we relax, we share stories about being crammed in the van. On our way to *no man's land* generally, the burbs, or worse, alongside the lake in Burlington, across from the ever-spewing chimneys, and we joke about trying to squeeze money from the very ones who slave away in these pollution factories and whose doors we mightily suspected would open to reveal three-headed dogs and cloven-hoofed children with cleft lips and Stepford wives and men with green flesh and metal plates in their brains and returning again and again to the subject of Eileen and how, through thick and thin, she'd jump into the van at the end of an evening and show us her six or eight new memberships while we'd be counting our silver to see how close we came to quota. Meanwhile, it'd be a race back to the city as over our shoulders we'd take a final peek at the lake, which appeared to be on fire beneath the factories' harsh glow.

The party's almost over and four of us remaining: me, Ray, Shelley and Simon so I figure I may as well let them in on what's happened with my book and all. They look at me a bit stunned, which I'm getting used to by now, no one quite believing, and, on the one hand, I can't blame them, but there's a difference here – it's as if I just farted or something. They turn and check each other's reaction. Finally, Simon smiles and says: way to go, Vic. Only it's not his big, goofy smile, it's more restrained. And Shelley says: yeah, congratulations. And Ray goes: yeah, good on you. I sense the tension and say, hey, it's early, how 'bout we go next door to the Madison for a few more drinks. My treat. Simon begs off with a prior engagement and Shelley has to study "goddamned" Hamlet. Ray has to get home to the wife. Another time, I say, and they all nod. The other two leave and Ray motions me aside.

"I guess I can assume you won't be into work on Monday."

"I'm not sure yet. I think, maybe Monday is OK."

"I don't think it's a good idea," says Ray.

"What do you mean?"

"Face it," he says. "You don't need this job now. You've made it. If you show up, you won't be able to concentrate. You won't have your heart in it. And neither will anyone else. No one will make quota and that costs the organization money. The brass are already on my back about whether or not the canvass is a viable proposition."

Ray makes quotes in the air with his fingers.

"They want to kill the canvass?" The rumour's been spreading for months and everyone's on edge, thinking it could never happen, at the same time wondering what they'd do if it did go belly up. As I say, the place provides the only work some of them can manage.

"Yeah. So, like I say, maybe it's better. I can call in one of the spares. You understand, right?"

"Sure, Ray. Sure. I understand. Maybe I'll just show up later and meet a few of them at the pub."

"Yeah. Maybe. Thanks, Vic. All the best."

I do understand. Together with the shock of Eileen's death comes the further shock that I've made it, I'm getting out, I've achieved what the others can only dream of, and no matter that we're buddies and they want to be happy for me, there's no shaking the fact that they're stuck. If I had won a thousand bucks in the lottery or even a new car, they could react in a more open, friendly and caring manner. This was a trip to the stars and beyond. In a certain odd way, it's the same as dying. There's no going back. It's as if I've betrayed them.

I turn from the office and spin around to the pub. I go upstairs. I sit by myself at the bar and order a glass of red wine. I watch the ball game. Jays are playing New York just as they always have, just as they always will. Except now it's Hudson on second base instead of Alomar, Delgado on first base instead of – I can't recall. And that's just the way it is. Just the way it always will be. Everything different, yet everything the same. Like a snake shedding an old skin.

Soriano drives the ball deep...

5

Sic itur ad astra: Such is the way to the stars

The usual office squalor: books overflowing shelves onto desks, chairs, cardboard boxes, plastic milk crates, floor; manuscripts piled either to be read or to be worked on or to be sent back as *thanks for thinking of Vigilante but not really our cup of poison*; scattered stacks of miscellaneous papers: contracts, promotional material, order forms, letters; a few plants that somehow manage to survive through the dust, the mildew, the reek of printer's ink that accompanies each fresh shipment, the cigarette smoke; the too-small garbage cans spilling paper cups, cellophane wrappers, half-eaten sandwiches, orange peels; a "cans and glass only" recycling box in dire need of emptying; a portable radio hidden somewhere behind the chaos barely coughing out FM 102.1 *the edge* through the static; Kevin crushing another cigarette stub into what may or may not be an ashtray; mousetraps, cockroach motels...

"You're on your way," he says, handing me a cheque. "Lucky bastard. Soon it'll be a condo in the Beaches and dinners at

The Four Seasons anytime you want. Did you ever see so many zeros?"

"What about you? You'll be pulling stakes for swank digs in Yorkville, complete with filtered water cooler, wet bar and espresso machine."

"Yeah, right. What with the Chapters/Indigo fiasco and distributing companies going belly up and Istvan Tarnoc chewing my ass and no one interested or barely able to read a book these days, this'll just manage to dig me out of the hole and keep me afloat long enough for the next disaster. Such as when the various arts councils get wind of this. They'll not only want to cut my funding, they'll be demanding I give back what they gave me previously."

"Never fails – what the lord giveth, the lord taketh away, tenfold."

"Amen, brother."

"I'm thinking the movie should help boost book sales, yeah? Earn a few extra bucks."

"Totally. Speaking of which, I've got more big news. You've got a one-way ticket to Tinseltown, yeah? After that, you spend a couple of weeks on the road doing the promo thing, ending in Chicago with – guess what? An interview on Oprah. That alone should sell another fifty to a hundred thousand books."

"I thought she stopped the book club."

"The word is out, pal. You're the new flavour. Should last about –" Kevin snaps his fingers, "*that* long, so take advantage. My advice to you? Whatever they say, just nod politely: yes, boss; right, boss; anything you say, boss. If they tell you to jump, ask how high. If they ask you to bark like a dog, ask what kind. If they want to know whether you floss, you say absolutely, four or five times a day." He flips his wrist. "Shit, I gotta go. Another fucking meeting with another fucking lawyer. See you in a month or so and we'll have that drink."

"Yeah," I say to Kevin's back flying out the door. I follow

close behind, signal Cheryl and Norm with a slight wave. Cheryl nods, Norm makes with the thumbs up and, that's it – I'm gone, I'm outta there. I'm off to la-la land; trading snow for sunshine and gloves and boots for shorts and sandals.

Arrived in LA, I'm greeted by a limo and taken straight to the plush offices of Sid Norman, head honcho of Sid Norman Enterprises, which serves as umbrella for Sid Norman Productions, which oversees Sid Norman Films, which is affiliated with Sid Norman Talent Group and the Sid Norman Casting Agency, all of which I gather from the embossed sign at the entrance.

I don't know what it is with me, but I always have a funny feeling about people whose family name is also a first name. I don't quite trust them. Not axe murderers necessarily, it's been my experience that they tend to lean heavily toward the desperately needy and/or even schizo side of the personality scale, constantly seeking general love, attention and approval. Which maybe works out for the best in Hollywood, my conception being that everyone is either trying to become someone else or is being urged or forced to become someone else in one way, shape, or form. Though not much different from Toronto, I suppose. Scratch the surface of any waiter or waitress, taxi driver or lawyer, even, and you'll discover a wannabe actor, screenwriter or stand-up comic.

I suss out the secretary as she waves me through: youngish, attractive, shapely, pert, smartly dressed, immaculately rouged, painted, manicured and powdered, a folded copy of *Entertainment* magazine on her desk. Beside it, a thumbed pile of similar material: *Fashion, People, Vogue, Cosmo, The National Enquirer*. Beside these, a plastic container of dental floss and a bottle of spring water. Definite starlet ambitions. Or does she already do double duty appearing in Sid's films? Picture her topless, a gash across her pretty neck, blood cascading down her naked chest, shrieking.

Scratch the surface and discover more surface.

Sid is in his mid-sixties, I hazard, slight build, fit, tanned, average height, big smile, talkative. In other words, the present-day stereotype of an LA mover and shaker. He grips my hand and goes right into his spiel – how much he enjoyed the novel, how he's looking forward to making the movie, who he has planned to star, and drops names like Ben, JLo, Mel, Bobby, Kevin, Jodie (though Jodie sounding tied up at the moment, under contract, but not necessarily, definitely interested and my people talking to her people, so, working on it), possibly Uma and, speaking of which, Quentin on the horn wanting to direct, almost begging, and, who knows, maybe, unsure about the fit, yet – why not? Sid's gut telling him Ridley or Steven, who are also keen and perhaps a lighter touch, a better handle on the subtleties. The main thing being the right people for the right job, yes? Nothing half-assed.

I listen to Sid and consider – is this the same guy who's known for Grade B hacker films and is he bullshitting me or what? The "subtleties"? His last flick was titled *Night Screamers: The Revenge* wherein a group of zombie cheerleaders rise from the grave with the bloody-minded purpose of avenging themselves upon several 'members' (pun intended) of a college football team who drugged, raped, murdered, then buried the girls' bodies beneath the fifty-yard line of the home team playing field. Promo: *What are those strange sounds emanating from the stadium after dark and why is everyone afraid to work the night shift?* The movie culminates with the young women performing a grisly dance routine employing the heads and genitals of the gridiron stars.

I don't know what sort of puzzled look I must've had on my face, though something of a question mark for sure, and dead obvious, as it registers easily with Sid.

"This is a real opportunity for me to jump up in class and

play in the big leagues for a change. We're talking Oscar winning material here. Oh yes, you wouldn't believe the people calling me about this picture. And not simply the industry types, oh no – celebs, stars, folks that normally wouldn't be caught dead beside me in a coffee shop."

He mimes holding a phone. "Hello, Sid? It's me, Harrison. I understand you're shooting that hot new film based on that hot new underground novel by that hot new Canadian novelist. Just want to let you know that I'm available. Let's talk. Soon. We'll do lunch. My tab. *Click!* Hello, Sid? It's me, Catherine. Michael and I just adored your last film. It was so...gothic. We understand you're casting *The Long Drive Home* and we want you to know that we picked up the novel and read it and loved it and feel we'd be perfect for the husband and wife leads. I mean, after all, we *are* husband and wife, yes? I'll leave my personal cell number. Call. Anytime. Or, better yet, drop by the house. Dinner, yes? Soon. Ciao. *Click!* Hey, Sid, my man. It's me, Denzel. I hear you need a black dude to add some colour to your white-ass script. Detective brother or whatnot. Shit man, I can do that role in my sleep. Put on twenty pounds, take off twenty pounds, whatever. You call me, dig? *Click!* Hello, Sid? It's me, Dusty. *Click!* Hello, Sid? It's me, Gwyneth. *Click!* Hello, Sid? It's me, Salma, it's me, Demi, and so on and so on. It never stops. You think I'm shitting you. Take a look at this."

He shoves a letter in my face. "This is an invitation to the biggest bash of the year. Hef's Playboy Mansion party. You don't get this unless you've made it. And, my boy, we've made it. It's tonight after eight. I'll have the limo pick you up at your hotel at a quarter to. Don't say you have nothing to wear, a tux has been ordered and waits for you in your room. Any questions?"

"Just one," I say, only slightly bewildered. "How did you manage to get hold of my book in the first place?" After all this other pure fantasy-come-true, I wonder how close the reality had been to my original convolutions involving the secretary and such.

"Oh, the usual channels."

"Usual?"

"Yes. Through the agency I deal with. They contact me if they find anything I might be interested in. I had told them I wanted something...a bit more...a bit more..." He struggles with the words; waves his hands through the air.

"A bit more...?"

"Exactly!" He points a finger at me, grins, snaps at his assistant. "Take Mr. Stone to his hotel. Make sure he's comfortable. I've got a million things to do. You wouldn't believe it. See you tonight. We'll talk."

So much for that, I think, and what does it matter *how* anyway? The main thing is, it happened, it's happening, and later tonight I'll be once again slipped through the rabbit hole and bundled off in a carriage to visit the sparkling, magical land of plaster of Paris grottoes, silicone breasts and cotton bunny tails.

Well, well, said Alice, one pill makes you larger.

The crowd at the Mansion is everything I've ever imagined and more, with everyone packed in like the proverbial sardines and sliding through the throng as if following invisible currents, an appetizer in one hand, a drink in the other and eyes on the lookout for anyone who needs an elbow bumped, a back patted, a waist wrapped or a cheek kissed. I begin with Sid but he loses me in about a second and a half. There's Jerry, he shouts. I'll leave you to mingle. He's off in a flash and I'm left to manage on my own. Which is fine by me, as *mingling* is not my bag, preferring to wander quietly alone, enjoy a glass of wine and take in the festivities from a distance. Well, a rather close distance in this case as everyone is hip to jowl.

For lack of any stimulating conversation, there is certainly enough eye candy so as not to become bored. Bunnies and assorted female company alike are arrayed in various forms of dress or undress ranging from head-to-toe period piece costumes with obligatory bodice overflow to full naked body paint illustrating either foliage, animals or outerwear (shades of Demi Moore's *Vanity Fair* cover) to squares and patches of cloth or strings of jewellery or metal chains or feathers or fur or hair covering the naughty bits (or revealing the naughty bits, depending) to stark naked except for heels used to *accent-u-ate* the positive – long, slim legs and round, smooth, tight asses.

The men, typically, are more or less clothed, though many (most) still give reign to some modicum of indecency or *regardez-moi* attitude: the faux punk, goth, street or grunge look, the flashy, open-buttoned, chest-revealing shirts, the meticulously planned mismatches: clash of fabrics, stripes with checks, uncoordinated colours: brown shoes with black pants or white socks, expensively tasteless gold chains, Rolex watches, *nouveau* tattoos, body rings, diamond-embedded incisors – *Bling! Bling!* – sunglasses indoors ("I have sensitive eyes." Sure. And that white powdery stuff on the end of your nose is icing sugar, right?), fresh-from-the-salon freaky-deaky hair styles, Armani, Versace, Hugo Boss, Homer Simpson. I have no idea what I'm draped in. I can merely assume that it's pricey and has some kind of designer *name* attached to it.

All in all, a bit sad, really, this portrayal of upper-class herd mentality. Everyone desiring and attempting to be different, meanwhile caught up in the same rut; the same fashion *non*-sense. Yet, whether inside or out, difficult not to be impressed, ultimately, in a circus-y sideshow sort of way. I mean, it's not as if these folks aren't of age, intelligent and aware of what they are doing, 'cause it's only too clear they are. No one could come up with this much weird shit strictly by accident, it has to be painstakingly thought out and implemented. So much the worse when there must be numerous other better and more valuable ways to spend one's time, effort and money.

Though, maybe not, and who's to say? After all, I'm a stranger here myself.

Which raises a cogent point. There is an inherent problem with deciding to be an observer rather than a participant in such grand affairs as the Playboy Mansion party. One is quickly regarded as suspect and certain tall, brawny, thick-necked, wide-browed, narrow-eyed men dressed in black, wearing headsets, likely packing (whom I assume are/must be house security and/or henchmen), have been zeroing in on me and are now gathered in a whispered discussion complete with quick glances in my direction. The host himself enters at the perimeter of the action. With his signature head of unruly silver hair and clad in a set of pressed, baby blue pyjamas, smoking the ubiquitous pipe, a pair of blonde beauties curved sinuously around each arm, he appears elegant; almost regal. He encroaches upon the tight fist of men. More whispering and quick glances ensue. He smiles as he strides toward me. He removes the pipe from his mouth and extends a hand.

"Good evening. I'm Hef. I don't believe I've had the pleasure."

Charming and gracious, I venture, though not without sensing something of an air of a good old boy traffic cop who pulls you over for no other motive than to check your ID, then proceeds to have you empty your pockets, open your trunk, clear out your back seat, count backwards from a hundred by sevens. Can't be too careful now, can we? What the hell, I might be a gatecrasher for all he knows, a terrorist, armed and dangerous with a six-pack of explosives strapped to my waist or a vial of toxic chemical stuck up my rectum.

Might be, but I'm not. This fact of my innocence notwithstanding, as with every encounter I've had with an authority figure, my temperature rises, my flesh sweats, my skin reddens and I begin to question the validity of my presence in this place; among this company. If I tell him who I am, will he be familiar with my name? Why should he be? I'm certain he has his *people* draw up the guest list. What if it was a mistake? What if he intended to invite Sharon Stone, not Victor Stone? Unlikely, but not impossible. Perhaps the best thing is to say I'm a guest of Sid Norman. Then again, who the hell is Sid Norman among this swank group? He as much as said so himself: *Not in the same league. Mea culpa, mea culpa, mea culpa.*

Mr. Hefner remains extremely patient as I consider my response. Meanwhile, the men in black inch closer.

"I'm here with...I mean, I arrived with...I mean, I'm a guest, or...not so much a *guest* exactly, as an associate of...that is...Sid Norman, the film producer...he and I, we're...well, he... Actually, I'm just..."

"Ah, you must be Victor Stone. I'm sorry I didn't recognize you, the photo on your book jacket doesn't do you justice. Or perhaps it's the light. At any rate, I've been looking forward to meeting you. You've come highly recommended. I didn't realize you'd be so modest." He turns to his entourage. "Ladies, gentlemen, this is Victor Stone, the brilliant novelist, soon to be brilliant screenwriter, I was telling you about. As all of you are aware, I draw up the invitation list for this little soiree personally over a period of several months in order to ensure that I have the *crème de la crème* attend. Normally, I'm booked to the limit weeks before and I'm not in the habit of making last-minute changes or adding names beyond a given number. But, as soon as I heard that Victor Stone would be in town, I knew I had to throw propriety to the wind and be the first to congratulate him and extend a warm, grand Hollywood welcome. After all, what's the difference whether one thousand or one thousand and one? Especially when the one thousand and first is the new, hot, rising star, Victor Stone."

"That's very kind of you, Mr. Hefner, but..."

"Call me Hef. Everybody does."

"Um, OK. Sure."

"Hef," he repeats.

I nod. I don't know what it is, but I can't bring myself to say the word. Maybe it's because it's been made into such a cliché in the movies. That is, to go through this inane routine: "Thank you for everything, Mrs. Smith." "Please, no need to be so formal. Call me Emily." "All right...Emily." There's a chord of sappy music and the audience is expected to somehow swallow the notion that the use of the given name immediately breaks the ice and the two become fast friends, or lovers, or accomplices to murder.

As if.

Or maybe it's because I think it's such a forties or fifties thing. *Spanky, Sparks, Biff, Happy.* Maybe it's deeper than that. Maybe it's because I've always had trouble in the past using nicknames or odd shortenings of names or initials. I mean, calling someone *Bear* because they're sort of big and hairy, or Peg instead of Margaret, or J.C. instead of Jesus Christ. It's almost sacrilegious. Not always, naturally, since I don't mind being called Vic, myself. Maybe it's simply a matter of needing time to get used to it; to adjust. Maybe it's the feeling of being in over my head at the moment. Him saying all those nice things about me and he's Hugh Hefner for Chrissakes. I cut my voyeuristic teeth as a boy thumbing through my dad's cache of *Playboy* magazines. How can I call him *Hef*?

"Are you having a fabulous time? Meeting people? The stars are out tonight. I'm sure several would enjoy making your acquaintance. Meg is here. Bruce. Catherine and Michael. Kevin. Tom. Don't be afraid. They won't bite. Have another drink." He signals to a waiter who replaces my empty glass with a full one. "Relax. That's all you have to do now. Relax. Feel free to take a tour of the premises." He tilts his chin, squints and directs the stem of his pipe at a spot on my mouth. "You have a piece of, I believe, celery lodged between your teeth, there. You'll find dental floss in every bathroom. Help yourself. Remember, my house is your house. You are always welcome here." He clenches the blondes and sails off into the fray. *Brad!* he calls. *Jennifer!* I scan the room. What is it with this first names business? A few I can understand immediately. There aren't that many Demis or Quentins around, fine. Others I can put into context: Catherine and Michael, OK. But aren't there a number of Kevins of note in the biz? Off the top of my head I can name Kevin Spacey, Kevin Costner, Kevin Bacon, Kevin Kline. How do they know which one they're talking about? How do they understand each other? Or is everyone so tuned in? Or is everyone so interchangeable? I'm the new, hot novelist, though I may not ever write another novel. I'm the new, hot screenwriter, though I've never written a screenplay and likely never will. I'm the new, hot, rising star and we know what happens to those. What did Kevin say? Whoops, there's that name again and no one in this vicinity thinking of my publisher when I say it. I snap my fingers. *That* long. So take advantage.

After a couple more drinks I wind my way down into the belly of the beast – the famous grottoes, to see if the reports are true. They are, somewhat, meaning, there are numerous folks gambolling nude in the tumbling, brightly-lit waters. No one famous, of course. Whether fear of secret videos and scandals or too déclassé for the nouveau ultra-rich, ultra-bored, or not wanting to get their outfits wet; ruin their makeup, I don't know. Best guess is that it's simply not the most advantageous environment in which to be *seen* making the *scene* whereas upstairs...

I even suspect that the fresh, nubile bodies on display are just that – employees paid to provide low-grade provocative entertainment for anyone who ventures forth, allowing for some semblance of sexual freedom and debauchery without the risk. Theatre. More, then, for the *pretense*, the pleasures of the eye rather than the body. Which is in keeping with the Playboy philosophy, after all. The naked figure artfully rouged and powdered, decorated and posed, skilfully lit, shot through a filter, finally airbrushed and glossed over in order to remove any further blemishes and imperfections. The result being an image meant to be adored, honoured and revered. Sexual, yes, but innocent. The girl next door. The prom queen. Within sight, yet, forever out of reach. A girl/woman who escapes every physical contact; who can only be obtained through fantasy and the erotic machinations of the male psyche.

Not that I believe for a moment that people don't get laid here. I'm positive they have and they do. It's simply not as blatant and ongoing as the stories and gossip magazines would have us believe. Moreover, I'm sure there's some sort of rites of passage or secret handshake or set of rules or governing laws or shibboleth (*Hef,* I murmur. *Hef, Hef*...not half-expecting the walls to tremble and collapse, reveal multiple open-invitation orgiastic scenes straight out of *Caligula,* but no...) that those in the loop observe and follow and which the rest of us are not privy to and which we will never be privy to for whatever closely guarded reasons. Certainly, for all the spirited spectacle of flawless flesh and possible promise of promiscuity before me, I do not expect to be ardently accosted or even awkwardly approached by one of these beautiful bunnified, bounteous beauty babes, never mind literally lasciviously laid.

Oh my God, I must be getting drunk. I'm pontificating. Worse, I'm alliterating. Badly. As well as puns. *Bunnified*? That's terrible. I lean an elbow against a sign on the wall that reads: FOR YOUR SAFETY, THE SAFETY OF OTHERS AND FOR GENERAL HEALTH CONCERNS AND PROPER POOL MAINTENANCE, **PLEASE** ADHERE TO THESE SIMPLE RULES: Shower before entering the pool. No strongly scented personal hygiene products. No drinks or food in the pool. No urinating in the pool. No smoking. No drugs. No pets. No running. No shouting. No balls or toys of any kind. No inflatable equipment. No transistor radios or other electronic devices. No cameras. No condoms. Do not harass the bunnies. Do not feed or disturb the fish. Kindly put all litter in containers provided. Remember, a clean pool is a happy pool. Thank you for your cooperation. Enjoy!

That sums it up, I figure. That says it all. Welcome to the new millennium, *Hef.* Everything laid out lean, clean and mean. Time to stumble back upstairs and procure myself another drink.

"Hi there!"

Oh my God, oh my God – it's one of the beautiful bunnified nubile nymphs glowing wet and naked in front of me. She has long blonde hair, big blue eyes, dimpled cheeks, a smile like a white picket fence and breasts that resemble a pair of fattened doves. Her nipples stand at cool, crisp attention, water drops clinging to each delicious, pinky-brown nub. Is it live, or is it Memorex, I wonder? I figure her for about eighteen or nineteen.

"Hi, yourself," I grin.

"My friend over there says that you're John Malkovich. Are you John Malkovich?"

I in no way even approximate John Malkovich. OK, I'm balding and there is the nose, but...seriously, no. I decide she wouldn't know John Malkovich if he came up to her lisping Shakespeare and bit his initials into her left tit.

Which reminds me of a terrific story involving Leonard Cohen. He's at the Chelsea Hotel way back when, drunkenly searching the halls for Nico, whom he's mad for. Janis Joplin is simultaneously drunkenly searching the halls for Kris Kristofferson, whom she's mad for. She bumps into Leonard and asks him: Are you Kris Kristofferson? Leonard asks: Have you ever seen Kris Kristofferson? Janis says: No, I've only heard him, but I know he's staying here. Leonard says: Well, you're in luck. I'm Kris Kristofferson. They end up in the sack and it's Janis who was "giving me head on the unmade bed" in the song 'Chelsea Hotel #2.'

Or is this mere apocrypha? Whatever. In other words,

I could say, yeah, I'm John Malkovich and see where it leads. Except, I can't. I can't say that. In very base Shakespearian terms (no lisp, but a noticeable slur) I can't *lie* to her in the hopes of *laying* her. It's not in me; not in my nature, either drunk or sober.

"No," I say. "Sorry. I'm not John Malkovitch."

Shit, I wince, the possibility of *country* matters fading in the mist.

"Oh," she says, and twists her mouth, slightly saddened, *boo hoo*, though not entirely dissuaded. She brightens and throws out her breasts. "Well, are you anyone famous?"

I shake my head. "No. Afraid not."

Shit, I wince again.

"Hmm." She shrugs her shoulders and her breasts kind of bob. "Too bad," she grins.

"Yeah," I say. "It is too bad."

The last I see of her is her lovely white ass followed by the bottoms of her lovely white feet disappearing into the lovely blue pool, *in puris naturalibus*: quite naked.

Right, I go. So much for that. I give my head a shake. Shakespeare? Where the hell am I digging this stuff up tonight? Why isn't Kim here to take my hand and guide me through this maze? This *a-maze*. We could have some fun. Yikes! Better track down a waiter before I get too nostalgic. Next thing you know I'll be wishing I was back home in the shivering night rain having doors slammed in my face in the middle of *dis*-respectable Willowdale canvassing for Friends of the Ecology; having to bear the not-so-sweet sounds of yapping dogs and crying children, the blare of TV sets from living rooms and the pitched voices of angered middle-class suburbanites in doorways growling, "Garbage problem? What garbage problem? We put our garbage out twice a week and in the morning it's gone. No problem."

Go back to that? Ha! Not bloody likely.

It's next morning and Sid wants to introduce me to the writing team. Not *introduce* exactly. Meet. Not even. Stick my head in and nod.

"Hey everyone! This is Victor."

There must be a dozen of them circled around a large table covered with laptops, pens, pencils, piles of paper, coffee mugs, water bottles, juice containers, remnants of cheese danishes, muffins, bagels. At a glance, a nice *PC* mix of folks: men, women, black, white, yellow, someone in a wheelchair, another who appears to be a man with long red hair, red nail polish and breasts. He waves a fat hand. The *team* interrupt their discussion to give me the two thumbs up and a litany of encouraging words: Brilliant. Fantastic. Genius. Don't worry. The screenplay writes itself. Piece of cake. With kid gloves. You'll never know. Won't change a thing. Relax. Trust us. Et cetera.

The door shuts.

"You see what I mean? They love you. They love the book. The thing is, we're working to a deadline. A very tight deadline. We need to have it ready to premiere this year at Cannes. It's already been accepted. The first few scenes have been written. Most of the roles have been cast. Rehearsals have begun. We've yet to decide on a director. Not a matter of finding, you understand, but of which one from a large number to choose. Who will it be? Someone with a proven track record, someone in mid-career needing that one big break, someone hot off a first hit or someone relatively unknown or totally unknown; a dark horse? Maybe we should let them fight over it, huh? What do you say? Place them in an arena, give them knives, swords, spears and let them go at it, huh? Last one standing gets the job. I think the set's still around somewhere from *Gladiator*. Be great fun, don't you think?"

"This has all happened since yesterday?"

"What do you mean *yesterday*? This has all happened since this morning. Would you like to take a peek? We're doing set-up shots in the studio today. Interiors. Out of sequence, you understand. The restaurant scene with the two detectives and the waitress. That bar scene where the detective sells the Glock to the lawyer. The kitchen with the unfaithful husband and the unfaithful wife. Nothing fancy, of course, but you'll get the general idea, see a few of who's on board. Thing is, there's no time for a lot of idle chit-chat, if you get my drift? We get in, we get out. To give you a heads up, and so as there are no surprises, I should warn you: you may discover there's been a few changes here and there. This is not uncommon and I'm sure you're aware. Film is a different medium than the printed word. You're a smart guy, so you know that. Nothing to do with the integrity of the book. Nothing whatsoever. Basic Film 101. Cut to car, cut to house, cut to highway; close up, fade, and so on. Boring, but necessary. Move the story along. Let the actors do their job, yes? The thing is, we're working with professionals here. You have to trust the process. Am I clear?"

I nod, sure, and away we go.

Relegated to the back of the set and trying to catch a glimpse through the layers of film equipment, I put on my glasses and – sonofabitch – if it isn't Chris sitting at the table with Mark and being served by *what's her name* – Mena? Is that it? So much for a waitress with bad complexion and buckteeth. In another corner, Ben and JLo are having a tête-à-tête with Salma, who I must assume is playing the horse-faced woman and Kevin, who can only be the formerly sweaty, pudgy lawyer gone Club Med. Well, well, I go: the more things change. Sid's been hunched over his cellphone. He folds it, grabs me by the arm and muscles me toward the door.

"Change in plans," he says. "More venues have been added to your itinerary. You're to be in San Fran to do a radio show tonight. Then it's Salem, Seattle, Denver, Albuquerque, Dallas. The list goes on. Word is definitely out. They need you to hop a cab to the hotel and pack up, my boy. Tickets and an updated schedule will be there when you arrive. Nice to meet you. All the best. Sorry you couldn't stay longer, but that's showbiz." He gives me a final push onto the sidewalk and hails a cab. I jump in. "The Sheraton, driver, and be quick about it. So long, Victor. By the time you're back in Toronto this one will be in the can. In the *can*, get it? The *Cannes* Film Festival."

The *can*, I think. Yeah, I get it. Except (and maybe it's my cynical nature), I can't help imagining a different sort of *can* in which this film will eventually appear. Or disappear. I also can't help but wonder who they've lined up to play the older fascist/religious couple who manage the motel? Perhaps Brad and Jennifer, ha ha?

I shouldn't laugh. It's not funny.

What am I saying? Of course it's funny. It's hilarious. In fact, it's absolutely hysterical. After all, it's Hollywood: *reel* life, not *real* life. Nothing is as it appears, nor does anyone wish it otherwise. Put twelve monkeys in a room with twelve typewriters and let them bash away. In the final analysis, it's not the quality of the product that counts, but how the spin doctors package and serve it up to a generally lazy and undiscerning audience. In fact, seems the less story the better, as it just gets in the way of the action.

Ah, the things you think, Mr. Stone; the things you say. Good thing nobody's listening. Good thing nobody gives two shakes. Good thing the money's in the bank.

Chicago. I'm in the green room stretched out on the sofa, a cup of coffee in my hand, my eyes focused on the hanging screen where Oprah holds court among her faithful. She's speaking to a woman who's rebounded from a life of poverty and drug addiction to start up and run her own successful self-help magazine titled *Within Reach*, which features articles and stories about others who have changed their lives in a positive fashion and how they went about it. Typical rags-to-riches stuff (whether monetary or spiritual) and I can understand the mass market appeal. Folks are forever relieved by the knowledge there are others close at hand who are worse off and who have pulled themselves out of the muck through a combination of their own bootstraps, the obligatory appeal to friends, family, God and prayer, plus inspirational messages from such top pop gurus as Tony, Deepak or even Oprah herself. Meanwhile, the nuts and bolts of the process are barely touched upon, if at all. I mean, who wants to hear that the woman worked for eight years in a box factory or spent four years in business school or inherited the start-up dough? No, rather believe that by pure force of will, God answered your prayers and the dark clouds parted.

I'm last on the program and due up next. There's just me and a female attendant.

"More coffee?" she asks.

"No thanks," I say. "I'm floating as it is. What do you make of all this?" I gesture with my chin.

"What?" she says.

"The woman being interviewed. The show in general."

She shrugs. "Oh, you know. I liked it better in the old days. People yellin' and screamin' at each other. Tearin' at each other. Everyone screwin' around with someone else. Husbands wantin' to kill their wives, wives wantin' to kill their husbands."

"Did that go on back here, as well? Offstage"

"Are you kiddin'? They were sweet as pie back here. Saved it all till they got in front of the camera, then, *wham!* All hell broke loose. It was funny. Now it's blah, blah, blah." She laughs. A light blinks. "That's your cue."

"Please join me in welcoming our special guest this afternoon, the writer of the novel and soon to be movie, *The Long Drive Home*, Victor Stone!" Oprah stands, flashes the book cover and leads the applause. I enter and take my place in a chair beside her.

"Thank you for joining us this afternoon, Victor, I've been looking forward to talking with you."

"Likewise. Thank you for inviting me."

"Not at all. Your novel, *The Long Drive Home*, is amazing. It's one of those rare books that, once you pick it up, you can't put it down. I read it straight through to the end over an evening."

"I appreciate your telling me. The sad truth is, most of the interviewers I've talked to so far hadn't taken the time to read the book. A few didn't even have a copy. They were basing their discussion on the press package and the hype."

"Well, I read the book and I loved it."

"Thank you."

"Not at all. Before we talk about the book, I'd like to ask you how your life has changed since you've been recently discovered?"

"It's hard to say. In many ways, I can't tell, it's all been happening so quickly. On the one hand, it's a total one-hundred-eighty-degree flip. On the other hand, not much has changed. I guess what's most interesting is that suddenly I'm a desired quantity; my name has cachet. People want to have me on their shows; they want to invite me to their parties. Same with my work. Poems that had been sitting with magazine editors for months are now being read. At least, I think they're being read. In any case, they're being accepted for publication. I had sent a small play to a theatre – I think it was two years ago, maybe three – and never heard a peep. Out of the blue, my phone rings – Albuquerque, New Mexico, of all places, and they want to produce it in their upcoming season. Having been ignored by the local Toronto media for years, I'm bombarded with invitations for interviews, discussions, photo ops, reviews, opinions. Meanwhile, I'm fully aware that the bulk of them don't know anything about me or my work. It's all due to my raised celebrity status around the movie."

"What do you say to all this? Do you feel resentful?"

"No, not really. I say sure, why not? I mean, I'd rather be lauded honestly for my writing, but at least the work will find a larger audience and, ultimately, this larger audience will decide whether it's worthwhile or not."

"And you think it's worthwhile."

"Yes. I suppose."

"Good. So do I. I understand you've been on a bit of a whirlwind promotional tour this past month. How's it going?"

"Pretty good, I think. I was in Hollywood, briefly, where I met some of the people involved with the movie. Then it's really been one city after another, signing books, speaking with various media types. Of course, most of them want to discuss the film aspect of things, rather than the novel. But, I have been getting reassuring messages that the book is selling well. Very well, in fact, especially since the news came out that I'd be on your show."

A card is flashed and the audience beaks into "spontaneous" applause.

"That's wonderful to hear." Oprah beams and nods her head to the audience. "There's been a fair amount of controversy regarding your take on the film and who's in it, is that correct? You're not pleased with the choices."

"It's not a matter of being pleased or not pleased. All I've said is that, the way the casting's been done, it's going to be a very different movie from the book. It has to be."

"But you also have been quoted as saying that the choices were made more for *star* status than for acting ability. Is that true?"

"I suppose. I mean, someone asks me a question, I try to be honest. In the end, though, it's just my opinion."

"The quote goes on to say that you laughed when the interviewer asked what you thought of the cast as actors."

"Again, it's just my opinion."

"Your opinion, yes. But, you're also the writer and a rising star yourself. That carries weight with the public."

"I wrote the novel. I've got nothing to do with the movie. They paid me to use the premise, what they do with it is up to them. That was the contract."

"I see. And your opinions, how do they sit with your producer, Sid Norman?"

"Sid? I have no idea. He hasn't been in touch with me."

"My sources inform me that he's not very happy. He's concerned that your views will have detrimental effects on the outcome of the movie."

"I don't think so. I'm one person. Meanwhile, there are millions of fans out there ready and willing to lay down their hard-earned dough to see the next big Hollywood blockbuster."

"You seem to have a very cynical view of both Hollywood and its audience."

"Oh no, it goes much deeper than that. Again, I know the only reason people are buying my book in the kind of numbers they are is because it's been picked up as a movie. And because I'm on your show. This immediately gives it a stamp of approval as a product that's *worthy*. It's a sort of bizarre blessing, which serves to open the door to folks who wouldn't normally touch my work with rubber gloves and a ten-foot electric cattle prod. I fully expect there'll be a group of people who have newly snapped up my book for this reason alone and who won't like it; will even hate it. Of course, they'll read it straight through to the end, because to put it down would admit some lack of intelligence or insight and set them outside the daily mass."

There are the beginnings of a slight stir among audience members, who lean in and whisper to each other.

"You have a very harsh view of the American public."

"It's not a harsh view. In fact, I've softened over the years. I used to say that ninety-five percent of everything that tried to pass itself off as art or entertainment or lifestyle or – whatever, you understand? of everything – was crap. Now I say that ninety percent of everything is simply mediocre, with maybe five percent being truly crap and five percent being the true goods, and, so, worthwhile. I mean, I'm merely pointing out the obvious here: that standards are set to the lowest common denominator in order to placate and/or control the masses. And I'm not blaming anyone per se, it's the system that's at fault. Rather than teaching us how to think, it teaches us what to think. Look in any daily paper and you'll notice, with few exceptions, the movies with the worst reviews take in the most revenue. Why? Because the media shoves it down our throats. What covers the walls of most homes and offices in a country as rich as North America is not original art but cheap prints of landscapes or knock-off movie posters. Gossip magazines with badly reproduced photos outsell literary magazines. Sports are a bigger draw than live theatre. World wrestling, dumb sitcoms and reality programs rule television. Soft rock insinuates itself into every elevator, office and telephone system. We elect the same morally bankrupt politicians and leaders over and over again. Everyone's content so long as the machinery keeps grinding away."

The crowd continues to show its agitation.

"I knew a woman once who told me about a professor of hers, who taught a university course in which he proclaimed that *Readers' Digest* magazine was a piece of pseudo-religious, propagandistic pap that served to brainwash its readership by dumbing down information, writing and literacy to such a degree that it was more insidious and dangerous than the atomic bomb, and, as such, should be banned from circulation. A tad radical, perhaps, but at the same time, it makes a certain amount of sense to me."

"You used the term pseudo-religious. It would appear from your comments and your writing that you also don't have a very high opinion of religion. Or God."

"Again, so far as I'm concerned, between God and religion, king and country – and maybe love – more wars have been fought, more atrocities borne, more murders committed than for all other reasons combined. To paraphrase Gore Vidal: whenever I feel the slightest urge to embrace God, I read the headlines of the morning paper. This quickly reaffirms my atheism."

"So, you don't believe in God?"

"What's to believe? You know that phrase, *Nothing is sacred*? I think, yeah, it is. It must be, since so many people are bowing and scraping to it rather than taking any personal responsibility for themselves or the world in general."

"I find your views rather odd, even alarming, given your recent good fortune. You've been blessed, Mr. Stone. Out of nowhere, your book was chosen; you were chosen. You've become a celebrity. You have an opportunity to make more money than you ever dreamed possible. Can you honestly sit there and tell me that you did this on your own?"

"I can't say I did it on my own, entirely. Certainly, there was some amount of luck involved and the circumstances had to be right for things to fall into place. I mean, it's happened to others before that they've been slaving away for years – Jack Kerouac, let's say – and finally, the big break occurs and everyone acts as if the person has exploded, a full-grown success, from the head of Zeus."

I make a *hmm* sound and chuckle.

"You find something amusing?" asks Oprah.

"I was just thinking about another friend of mine who gained some sort of notoriety recently. He was one of the so-called "language" poets." I make quotation marks in the air with my fingers. "He had been doing his thing for quite a while, publishing here and there to a more or less particular and elite crowd. Then, he put together a book of poems titled *me/you, you/me* that managed to cross over somewhat into the mainstream. What he did was create two separate civilizations. One group spoke a language that used the letters from the first half of the alphabet and the other group used letters from the second half of the alphabet, which necessarily eliminated a lot of words, like – "words" for instance, because the "d" wouldn't be available with the rest, right? Sentences would be choppy, naturally, with everyone sounding like Bizarro in the *Superman* comics. The point is, both groups used perfectly good English words so far as the reader was concerned, but neither group could understand the other, right?"

Oprah nods her head, unsure. The audience makes with the collective glare, like: what the fuck are you talking about? I go on.

"I mean, the two groups lived divided for centuries on opposite sides of a "mountain"." I again make with the quotation marks in the air. "What we would call a mountain and which one group called a "cliff" and the other group called a "promontory," OK? They lived near a "river" which translated to "fall" or "spout," depending on which side of the mountain you were on. You see?"

Oprah looks unconvinced and the audience members squirm in their seats, their assholes wound tight as clocks, prepared to sound the alarm.

"At any rate, the two civilizations eventually meet and, as these things are bound to unravel, rather than seeing how combining their two disparate languages would result in a greater knowledge and understanding of the world and offer an enrichment of life in general, a war breaks out between them and they kill each other off. The *in* joke was that, while it was ostensibly a war of words, it entailed absolute total bloodshed and annihilation – the sword being mightier than the pen, right? It was quite clever and hysterically funny as well. Which was probably its saving grace and a large reason for its success."

"I see." Oprah smiles her big Oprah smile. The audience

steams. "And what became of your friend?"

"Same old thing. He was presented with a plum job as a university professor where he's required to slave away composing papers, articles, reviews, to maintain tenure. He's had to give up poetry. A large publisher picked him up to turn out a novel, which was well written, but mainstream; not terribly inventive or exciting. Bestseller, of course. Won some awards. He has a second novel coming out in the fall or spring, I think. We don't keep in touch."

"Sounds like your friend is a success."

"I suppose, if that's what you want to call it."

"What would you call it?"

"I don't know. Hamstrung. Emasculated. Castrated."

The audience is visibly aghast. Oprah maintains her cool.

"It appears to me that your friend was chosen from among a large number of possible candidates. Wouldn't you call him blessed?"

"Blessed?" I laugh. "No. He produced something that was a bit of a well-constructed novelty and was promoted by his publisher as well as several folks in positions of power. That and a touch of good fortune. It's like I've been saying – right product, right place, right time. He happened to be picked as the *flavour du jour.*"

"You don't see God providing the good fortune?"

I shake my head.

"So, you firmly believe that all of this has come about due to your own hard work and by chance; that the hand of God is nowhere to be seen."

"It's just my opinion. Everyone else has the right to go out and believe whatever they want. Bow down to sacred rocks, smoke magic mushrooms, pray to green-skinned, two-headed Martians, for all I care. Whatever makes you happy."

I notice a real pulse in the audience, with more than a few members looking like they're getting ready to jump out of their skins. I check the clock and we're almost out of time. I wonder if the attendant in the green room is watching and what does she think? Like the good old days again? Fully expecting (hoping!) fists will fly, blood will flow, or is it still a lot of blah, blah, blah?

"Do you think this sort of attitude will serve you well when it comes time to publish your next novel or produce your next screenplay?"

"The point is, there won't be a next novel or next screenplay. That was it. I'm done with it. Finished."

"You're not serious? What do you plan to do?"

"Go back to writing poetry. Be happy living in obscurity."

"Do you think that's fair?"

"Fair? What do you mean, *fair*?"

"To simply take the money and run. Is that fair? After all, *they* have a vested interest in you."

"*They*? Who are *they*?

She motions with a hand toward the audience, which is literally champing at the bit.

"Your public."

"My public." I smile. "I don't have a public. They're just people who, for the most part, are quite willing and content to bend whichever way the wind is blowing."

An audible gasp emanates from the seats.

"So, no God and no discriminating public. Is that it? A mindless, soulless, mass. No better than cattle." She rises and steps into the crowd.

"I didn't say that. I was speaking in *general*."

"They mean nothing to you." Again, she makes with the sweeping motion.

"No, it's not that..." I fidget in the chair and lick my lips.

"And God means nothing to you. You have nothing to thank Him for. You've come all this way on your own."

"Look..."

"What is your stance on abortion, Mr. Stone?"

"Abortion? What does that have to do with anything?"

"What about illegal drugs, Mr. Stone? Cocaine, heroin, hallucinogens. Do you floss regularly? Are your armpits clean? Do you crumple or fold the toilet paper before you wipe?"

"Listen, I don't see..."

Too late. A woman explodes from her seat.

"Dirty commie heathen! Ingrate! Pig! Slime bucket! Baby killer! Druggie! While the rest of us slave away...!"

Another woman.

"I love *Readers' Digest*! I've had a subscription for over twenty years! Does that make me an idiot?"

Suddenly it strikes me – people are listening to me, actually hanging on my every word. Moreover, they are affected by the things I say.

A man. Two more men. Shouting.

"Ungrateful bastard! Treating us like cattle! Worse! What gives you the right, you...? Someone ought to teach you a lesson, mister! Filthy monster! Scum! Pagan! The Lord giveth and the Lord taketh away! You'll get yours! Repent, sinner." Other stronger words fly which I assume are being bleeped out across the airwaves.

Security rushes forward and keeps the pack at bay. A man pulls something from a coat pocket. It could be a gun, or a hand grenade, but it's a stiff leather eyeglass case. He rears back, heaves it and nails me smack in the mouth. *Pervert*, he yells. A smear of blood stains my shirt.

"You're as good as dead, Stone! Do you hear me? As good as dead!"

A guard grabs me and guides me offstage. At the rear door, a woman greets me with a kiss on the lips. The guard shoves her roughly aside. She grins as she rubs blood from her hand onto her cheek. It's the female attendant.

"Thank you," she says. "Thank you." Her grin is almost

maniacal. I'm led onto the street and into a waiting car.

Next stops: Cleveland, New York, Buffalo, Montreal...

6

Facilis est descensus Averni: The descent to hell is easy

A ton of messages await me at home: stack of envelopes in the mail box, answering machine flashing non-stop, e-mail backed up. Most of it not overly important. Mainly media based and already taken care of as they managed to track me down on the road. Various folks zeroed in on my newly acquired wealth intent on selling me useless shit or wanting me to donate to such-and-such a worthy cause. A short (though insistent) message from Kevin warning to be in his office tomorrow morning, ten sharp, come hell or high water. And of course, the clincher – a rather frightening note that reads, "You're as good as dead, Stone. As good as dead. Watch your back." It's signed, "A decent citizen." Something you'd expect to see done up in bold letters cut and pasted from old newspapers and magazines. Instead, handwritten in the neatest of script. Should I take the note seriously? You bet your sweet ass. There are a lot of crazies out there. Even scarier, there's no stamp, which means the envelope was delivered by hand.

I dial the police.

Naturally, a mechanical voice answers. "You have a choice of six languages... ," then, "You have ten choices... ," then, "You have five choices..." There is a further manual relay from person to person until I eventually get a voice mailbox telling me to leave my name, number, a short message, and someone will get back to me within twenty-four hours. Fine, except it may be too late by then. What are the stats on people who send threatening letters or make threatening phone calls? Was it seventy/thirty that they did act or seventy/thirty that they didn't? Or was that for something else entirely?

I leave the required information with the machine.

Watch your back, the note says. What the hell? I inch toward the window and peek into the night. Nothing but street lamps and rooftops. What's wrong with people? How come freedom of speech only applies when you toe the party line? I turn on the TV. It's the news. Bloodbaths everywhere. More suicide bombers in Israel. More sniper attacks in Iraq. More women and children hacked to death in Africa. More riots in the streets of Paris. In the good old US of A some guy is to be executed for murdering a couple of doctors who performed legal abortions. His comment? "I am happy to die. You will make me a martyr in the eyes of others."

In Canada, some politician gets nailed by a cream pie. That's it. That's as far as the terror report goes. The rest is death by accident or misadventure, a cat trapped up a tree, the Leafs vying for a playoff spot and the weather promising more of the same: wet, cold and blowing. So, OK, chances are I'm being pestered by some copycat creep who caught my act on Oprah and after another beer or two will return to watching *Hockey Night in Canada* or reruns of *Temptation Island* and forget all about me.

Chances are. Though what if it's someone who's followed me across the border? A born and bred redneck American patriot complete with crewcut, tattoo on his bicep that reads "Mom," a firm belief in the constitutional right to bear arms and a bible slipped into his jockstrap for safekeeping?

I flick off the TV, pour a glass of wine and put on a CD. Something upbeat and kind of goofy. Jimmy Buffett singing: why don't we get drunk and screw. Indeed, and why not? Perhaps an overly simplistic philosophy, but better than bashing heads in with baseball bats. I'll put the chain on the door, toss a frozen pizza in the oven, spend the evening in, and get a good night's sleep.

I take a final glance out the window. A single room light illuminates the house across the alley. A curtain quickly draws closed. Was that light on earlier? I go into a slight crouch and ease myself backward into the kitchen.

I'm sleep deprived and partially hungover when I enter the office.

"Hey!" I greet Cheryl and Norm. Don't they ever move away from those computer screens?

"Hey!" They nod and it's right back at it.

The office is one big room, and, to my right, Kevin's perched on a chair across from two suits who appear more than a little out of place sitting on the old, beat-up leather sofa. They have briefcases beside them and there are papers neatly laid out on the coffee table in front of them.

"Kevin," I say.

"Vic. Good to see you. This is Michael and Lorna. They're lawyers acting for Venture Publications."

"Nice to meet you," we say in unison, and exchange handshakes. There's an uncomfortable silence as eyes dart person to person. Kevin begins.

"As you know, Vic just got back into town last night so I haven't had a chance to properly fill him in."

The two suits nod. "We understand. No problem. This is

more a polite formality than anything else. Paperwork. The rest, the more creative aspect, will be discussed with others further down the road. Simply a matter of signing a few documents and leaving the two of you to celebrate your good fortune."

"What's up?" I ask.

"Well Vic, it's great news, but sad news at the same time."

The suits keep nodding like a pair of bobble heads in a car window.

"What?" I don't like the way this is going. Kevin is normally up front and honest to the point of cruelty. It's not that he's a jerk, it's simply his manner and you either accept it or you don't, and move on. If you want it sugar-coated with a great big hug and a kiss, go home to Mommy.

"The bottom line, Vic – and we've been friends for years now, right? And I'm telling you as a friend, and I'm sure you'll understand that, given the circumstances, this is the best and maybe only possible decision – I mean, in fairness to everyone involved – What I'm trying to say is – your contract has been taken over."

"Taken over? What do you mean, *taken over?*"

The suits jump in as a single voice. "It means that you are now part of the Venture Publications family of authors. Congratulations. We merely need you to sign." They point at several spots. "Here, here, here, here and here. And here."

"I'm sorry to disappoint you folks, but I'm not signing anything. I'm not interested in being part of your family. Not even a third cousin twice removed. *Capiche?*"

"Perhaps we should tell you that, by law, we don't need your signature. We have merely provided these papers as a gesture of goodwill and to make sure that everyone understands what is required. As we said earlier, this is a polite formality."

"Am I missing something, or what?"

"You have no choice, Vic. I'm the only one who needs to sign, and I've signed. It's a done deal. It was in your contract."

"What was in my contract?"

"In the contract that you signed with me. It states that if Vigilante Editions is either unable to adequately represent an author, ie: filling book orders, providing proper media coverage and/or advertising, or if a second publishing company approaches with an offer that is deemed satisfactory, then the press can sell your contract to said buyer. I'm paraphrasing, but that's the nuts and bolts. It's standard in any contract. And as it stands, we can't keep up with the demand. We're too small."

"That can't be. Don't I have any rights here?"

"You signed those rights over to me. I told you to read the contract. I even offered to go over it with you."

"Yeah, but who'd have known? I mean, it sounds ludicrous. This is standard in any contract?"

The two suits nod.

"Listen, Vic. To be honest, the way you've been shooting your mouth off on tour, you should be happy that Venture still wants you. I mean, is there anyone you didn't manage to piss off?"

"Oh, that," the suits laugh. "A bit of controversy isn't such a bad thing. Book sales have taken a huge leap upward since the Oprah incident. Whether people are buying to see what the fuss is about or to use as kindling doesn't really matter. Naturally, from here on our people will work with you to make sure your remarks don't sail too far off the tracks. It's all been written in."

"Yeah? What else has been written in? The basics, I mean."

"Oh, nothing out of the ordinary. We decide who you see and don't see in terms of media. Eliminate the riff-raff. Keep to those who promote our authors and offer a list of questions ahead of time so that our specialists can prepare the most appropriate answers. You agree to be available to media and for special events and promotions from ten in the morning until ten at night seven days a week for the length of your contract, the length of your contract being five years, in which period we expect you to complete three novels. There are subheadings and sub-subheadings which are less important and which you can peruse in more depth later, should you wish. All very regular nowadays. Standard."

"I guess, except you're forgetting one very important detail." They stare blankly at me. "As I told Oprah, I'm through with novel writing. I don't have another novel in me. Not one."

The suits titter. "That's very amusing, Mr. Stone. You'll forgive us if we don't take the bait. You're a writer, and writers write. If it's a matter of writer's block." The suits make with the air quotes in tandem, grinning. "We're sure you'll get over it. After all, you're being paid enough."

"I'm a poet. I write poetry."

"Come, come, Mr. Stone. As much as we all admire poets and poetry, there's no audience, hence no money."

"I'm through arguing. I'm not signing anything, I'm not writing anything and I'm not going to be part of your family. That's final."

"We can take legal action, Mr. Stone. It's within our rights and within our powers to do so. We can sue you, and we will. Seven ways to Sunday. We'll take everything. Furthermore, we'll make sure you're never published again. You won't be able to write a poem on the toilet wall without us having it removed. Is that clear?"

"Sign the goddamn papers, Vic."

"No! You can take your papers and shove them up your collective arse."

"Can I talk to you?" Kevin ushers me into the hall. "Are you crazy or what? These guys are offering us a shitload of money. What is your problem?"

"My problem? Kevin, listen to yourself. Aren't you the one who refers to Venture Publications as *Vulture* Publications because they feed on small presses in order to eliminate the competition? Or they buy out writers once they begin to make it then turn them into corporate clones?"

"Yeah, I said that, but things have changed. They're being more than fair."

"I thought we were friends, and you're willing to sell me to the enemy like a piece of meat. What is that? What's happened to you? Is it the money? You need more, is that it? Fine. Take a bigger percentage. Sixty/forty? Eighty/twenty? Ninety/ten? Take it. I don't need much. Honest. I just can't agree to the terms of those bastards."

"Vic, I hear what you're saying, and I am your friend. Believe me. It's not just the money. Remember Istvan Tarnoc? I said he was a fucking psycho, making threats and whatever? Suddenly, he goes quiet. We don't hear a word from him and we figure maybe he's given up. Next thing you know, stuff starts to happen, strange and frightening stuff. Windows I know I've left closed, I return to find open. Doors that should be locked are unlocked. I go to my car and there are four flat tires. The phone rings at all hours and no one's there, the number can't be traced. I discover metallic devices with movable parts, timers and what appear to be sticks of dynamite strapped to them in the bedroom or bathroom with notes attached saying *If this were a bomb, you'd be dead right now*. I check my mail and there are envelopes that contain powdery substances. So far, none of them toxic or fatal. On top of this, Allanah has totally caved and is ready to go to court and admit that she plagiarized Istvan's work. Hell, she's ready to admit she blew up the twin towers single-handedly. I don't know what she's been through, she won't tell me. I can only assume that it's much the same as me. Maybe worse. To be honest, I fully expect to wake up one morning with a horse's head lying beside me in bed. So, you see, the situation is more complicated and complex than any of us realizes."

"OK, OK, if you wanted to scare me, you've done it. But what does Venture have to do with Tarnoc? He has a European publisher."

"How the fuck should I know? All I know is that once we began negotiating your contract, the big guns at Venture stepped in and were able to arrive at a deal with Tarnoc's lawyers where I cover the court costs, I pay to do another printing of Allanah's book where she credits Tarnoc, and I agree to publish his first novel for adults; hard cover, illustrated, medium-sized run."

"And you strike the letter 'R' from the alphabet," I mumble.

"What?"

"Nothing. Why does he want you to publish his novel?"

"Punishment. It's a piece of shit. Even his own publisher won't print it. It's going to cost me a small fortune."

"Did you call the police? See if they could do something? Implicate Tarnoc?"

"Are you kidding? Sure. They came up with a big, fat zero. Tarnoc's in fucking Hungary for Chrissakes tossing back vodka in the local bar. Can you imagine the type of network he must have to pull this off? Vic, we're in way over our heads here. There are powers at work that are beyond our comprehension."

"What if it's not Tarnoc?"

"Excuse me?"

"What if it's not Tarnoc? What if it's someone else?"

"Who else? Since I agreed to the terms, there's been nothing. Not a sniff. Take my advice and sign the papers. What does it matter? The reality is, you work for them now. There's no escaping that. The rest is a technicality. I mean, what's the worst-case scenario? They want three novels over five years? Fine. You don't have to guarantee the quality. Sit down over a weekend and write a totally shitty novel, hand it to them and they'll drop you like yesterday's garbage, right? Maybe you have to give back the advance – big deal. Like you say, you've got enough money already. Fuck 'em."

"Yeah, I guess. But why sign if I don't have to? If there's no real reason?"

"It's a technicality."

"A *gesture of good will* is what they said. Except I have no good will toward them. And they know it. And they don't care. It's all for show. They want the pretense of one, big, happy family."

"Still...As I said, they're willing to pay a shitload for it. You saw the figure, yes?"

"I saw. I'm impressed."

"But – "

"If I don't sign, what happens to you?"

"I've done my job – delivered the lamb to the slaughter. I collect my thirty pieces of silver, wash my hands and get on with my life. Which is what Allanah is doing and which is what you need to do. Come on, Vic! Look at the bright side – you're being paid to write. Get with the program. Go in, sign the fucking papers, I'll run out, pick up a bottle of decent Scotch, we'll drink, get drunk and by evening you'll have forgotten what it was you were so concerned about. OK?" Kevin has been waving his arms like a maniac for emphasis. He drops them to his side. "OK?"

"How did they know about Tarnoc and you in the first place? Did you tell them?"

"Aw, get real, Vic! I didn't need to tell them. Look, the publishing industry seems massive from the outside but, in fact, it's pretty small. And tightly knit. News travels fast. Especially bad news. They couldn't help but know."

"And they came to the bargaining table with this, the Tarnoc stuff, up front? You didn't ask them?"

"No. I mean, yeah. Pretty much. They offered."

I take a small step away from him, then another.

"What are you doing, Vic? Where are you going? Don't go. It's crazy. You can't escape this. It's impossible."

I reach the end of the hall. "I need time to think. Tell them I need some time. Until tomorrow. OK?"

I scoot down the stairs as the two suits stick their noses through the door frame.

"There's no time, you crazy bastard! Don't you understand that? The time has passed. It's over. It was over before it started. Vic?"

Kevin continues to shout but I don't hear him anymore.

Dark clouds and a bit of drizzle in the air. Reasonably mild without the wind. I eat a Tim Horton's muffin and coffee in the alley at back of my apartment building and check out the scene. What sort of shot does someone have and where is the best vantage point? My room is on the third floor of a four-level low-rise, meaning there is no opportunity from the parking lot unless I'm situated directly against either the bedroom or living room windows. A gunman moving further back of the lot extends the target area to about a third of the way into the rooms until he's stopped by the corner house. After that, it's either swing around the house and crouch in the street or climb a tree, all of which is pretty risky, from a *being caught* perspective. The best spot would appear to be from the house, either an inside window or the roof, the roof being ideal as almost at a level with my apartment. So, how get to the roof? An old aluminum tripod antenna is secured at the side of the house and runs bottom to top directly to the flat part of the roof. Perfect, I think. It's as if made to order for any lunatic with a rifle and no fear of heights. In fact, a ten-year-old kid with some gun savvy could probably scramble up, take aim, plug me with a bullet and scramble down in about the time it takes to crack a beer and pour it into a glass.

Perhaps a new place of residence is in order, methinks, and I hustle around front.

Another blank envelope has been slipped through the mail slot. The note reads, "Vengeance is mine, sayeth the Lord," and is signed, "A decent citizen." The difference is that, this time, the individual letters *are* cut and pasted from the pages of newspapers and magazines. I figure whoever's responsible got something straightened out in the interim. I guess he figured: Better late than never.

Upstairs, there are three messages blinking on the machine. Maybe one is the police. I hit the button.

"Hi, it's me, Kim."

Her voice is very stern and I get the distinct impression she's not calling to apologize or make up.

"What the hell do you think you're doing? If this is your idea of a joke, it's not funny. If you're angry at me, fine, take it out on me, not my family. Do you understand?"

Excuse me? Understand? Understand what? Second message.

"Vic? It's Kevin."

He's whispering. Why is he whispering?

"I know you're pissed off and I know this all seems pretty fucked up, but you've got to come back to the office. Now. It's the only way. I can't talk any more. Be careful."

What does he mean, he can't talk any more? Be careful of what? Message three.

"Hello, Victor. You don't know me, but I know you."

A voice using a bad *Chucky* imitation.

"An amusing message. What do you think of this one? Vengeance is mine, sayeth the Lord. You're as good as dead, Victor. As good as dead. Look out the window."

I think not. The phone rings. I pick it up.

"Yes?"

"What are you afraid of? Come to the window. Look across toward the roof. It's a better view than from the alley. I promise, I'll make it quick."

Jeezus! He must've been watching me the entire time I was outside. From where? From the sound, he's on a cellphone. I could slip out the front. Then again, what if he's lying? What if he wants me to think he's on the roof and he's actually waiting to nail me from across the street? Do I chance the back entrance? What if there's more than one of them? I catch a glimpse of my bed through a crack in the door. There's a metallic device the size of a shoebox sitting there with what looks like sticks of dynamite and a clock taped to it. He's been here. A shot rings out and my living room window shatters. Fuck! I grab my coat, charge down the steps, hurl through the door onto Bloor Street and burn rubber west. I'll grab some cash from the bank machine in the Annex and make myself scarce until I figure my best next move.

Yeah, as if I've figured any best moves so far.

I don't even know what the limit is for a cash withdrawal so reckon I'll err on the side of caution and punch in two hundred. The screen lights up: *Insufficient funds*. I know the cheque for half a million processed fine and there was no problem on the road, but I decide to lower my sights anyway. I hit one hundred with the same result. Impossible. I hustle over to a teller and ask what gives. She keys the card into the computer.

"According to our records, your account balance is three dollars and fifty cents."

"That's impossible. I took cash out a few days ago. There was plenty."

"The records also show that the account has been inactive for several years. Are you sure you're not thinking of another account? Savings perhaps?"

"This is the only account I have. There must be some mistake. I deposited a cheque for half million dollars over a month ago. I've been using the account."

"Do you have receipts?"

"I don't keep receipts."

She looks at me like I'm crazy and twists the monitor in my direction.

"As you can see," she says. "You might want to phone your home branch."

"OK, fine." I pull out my Visa. "Let's try this."

She flips the monitor, bangs some keys. Her head tilts and her face contorts. "Huh," she says, then steps back, grabs a pair of scissors and cuts the card into small pieces in front of me.

"What are you doing?" I choke.

"I'm sorry, sir, but the card is shown to be invalid and I've been requested to destroy it. You'll have to straighten things out with your main branch."

"But..."

"I'm sorry."

I'm stunned. How can this be happening? This can't be happening. This kind of thing doesn't happen in real life. It can't. There are rules; there are laws. This only happens in movies. I'm thinking David Lynch and *Mulholland Drive*. I'm thinking *The Game* with Michael Douglas. I'm thinking grand conspiracies. I'm thinking grave-looking men in dark suits driving up in black Cadillacs opening car doors saying, "Get in, we're going for a little drive." I'm thinking bodies dumped at the sides of deserted roads, floating in rivers, rotting in cheap motel beds or empty warehouses.

The teller's voice slices through the fog.

"Is there anything else I can help you with? Sir?"

I drag myself out of the bank. In my pocket, I count fifteen bucks, some change and two tokens. At the corner, a couple of guys stand talking. They catch me staring and laugh. I move up the street toward Spadina. I glance over my shoulder and almost trip over my own feet. The guys aren't following – they've disappeared entirely. I stop at a phone booth and drop in a quarter. I have to chance calling Kim and find out what's going on. What was she talking about?

"Yes?"

"Kim. It's me, Victor."

"Victor? Where are you? What's happening?"

"I was hoping you could tell me."

"Are you in trouble?"

"I guess."

"Well, you either are or you aren't."

"Then I guess I am."

"What sort of trouble?"

"No idea. I think it has something to do with the Oprah show but I'm not sure it isn't more than that. That message you left me, what was it all about?"

"I'm sorry about that. I know now it wasn't you."

"What wasn't me?"

"I got a message on my voice mail at work saying you were going to tell my kids about us. I thought you were getting back at me because I broke up with you."

"Do you honestly believe I'd do something like that?"

"I didn't want to believe it, but the voice sounded like you. He even called me *baby* the way you do. I couldn't help myself. I went nuts. Then I got another call. It was a woman this time. She said the first message was a warning and nothing bad will happen if I play ball."

"What? She used that phrase, *play ball*?"

"Yes. She said if I played ball, everything would turn up roses."

"She didn't say that? *Turn up roses*?"

"Yes. Why?"

"What else did she say?"

"She told me to wake up and smell the coffee. She said nice guys finish last. She said you have to break a few eggs if you want to make an omelette."

"Is this a joke? Was she trying to be funny?"

"It's not funny, Vic."

"Kim, don't you see?" I laugh. "She's using all these clichés in order to rib me? She's having her fun with me."

"What are you talking about?"

"The clichés."

"The clichés? I don't care about the fucking clichés. I don't want my kids to be the eggs in her omelette."

"I'm sorry. What does she want you to do?"

"She told me to tell you to wise up and give your head a shake."

"Gawd. OK. Anything else?"

"Floss."

"*Floss*? She wants me to *floss*?"

"That's it. She said you'd...capiche." Kim hesitates. I sense she's choking back a tear. "Vic, she also said to tell you...the phone is tapped."

"Christ!" I slam down the receiver.

7

Sentio aliquos togatos contra me conspirare:
I think some people in togas are plotting against me.

Chinatown. Early evening. A light drizzle in the air. Chilly. I'm wearing sneakers, jeans, undershirt, shirt, jean jacket, no hat, no gloves. All day I've been on the lam, keeping in heavy traffic, ducking in and out of malls and storefronts. I'm damp and getting damper. Around me, everyone appears suspicious; everyone is suspect. A little girl trains her baby blues on me and I immediately conjecture: midget, robot, hologram. A stroller slides by and I scan it for explosives. Trees and streetlights are rife with snipers. There is danger to be sniffed out everywhere; each object is capable of being transformed into a weapon. I move and I move and I move.

The point is, I can't keep moving forever. I know that. I'll have to sleep sometime. But how? And where? I caught a hot dog for lunch so I'm down to thirteen dollars and change. I slosh over to King's Noodle House, figuring I might bum a meal.

The place has been transformed. Brightly coloured ceramic tiles cover the old brick, the windows are spotless, there are no dead, crisp, BBQ'd ducks or pigs dripping from hooks. Peering through the glass, I see the entire place has been gutted and renovated. Above the door flashes a gaudy neon sign: *My-Tea Fine Noodles*. Who comes up with this shit? I notice Billy eating at one of the garish plastic tables. I hurry in.

"Billy," I say. "What's up?"

"Vic? What the hell you doing here? You in big trouble, yeah? You kill someone or what?"

"Why, what did you hear?"

"I don't hear anything. Just people come in and ask me questions."

"What people?"

"They don't say."

"Uh-huh. What goes here? I thought you had the place until the fall."

"Me too. Then I get a call. Some woman say she has company that wants to buy me out. I figure, sure, why not? Better than being thrown out, eh? They make me good offer."

"An offer you can't refuse."

"That's what she say. She talk like Tony Soprano. Pretty funny." Billy spoons his soup. "So, why you here?"

"I was hoping to bum a meal."

"Ha! I thought you told me you were rich."

"Someone screwed up."

"Sure. Someone always screw up."

"I guess. How's the food?"

"Lousy. Noodles mushy, broth has no flavour, chicken in little cubes."

"Then why are you eating it?"

"It's free. For next ten years I eat for free. All part of deal."

"But the food's lousy."

"Sure, lousy, but free. All I can eat." Billy slurps his soup. He talks with limp noodles clinging to his chin. "Oh, another part of the deal has to do with you."

"With me, huh. Let me guess. You're supposed to tell me to give my head a shake?"

"No. She say, if I see you, I'm supposed to give you this." He fishes in his pocket and pulls out a container of dental floss.

"What the hell?" I say.

Billy shrugs; tips his head past my elbow. "You know those guys at the door?" he says. "They come in right behind you. They been standing there watching us ever since."

I don't turn, I simply bolt for the back door.

Queen and Dovercourt. The starting point for a growing strip of small art galleries that stretches into Parkdale. The drizzle has let up. A few people huddle around cigarettes outside a storefront window. A poster in the window advertises the opening of an installation piece. I hustle inside to dry off and maybe take advantage of the obligatory cheese, crackers and crudités that habitually accompany such events. I fill a plate, do the obligatory polite tour of the space and its contents, grab more food and set myself down on a stool at the bar.

The exhibition isn't bad, with photos and structures that combine elements of the urban and rural landscapes: photos with passenger planes superimposed on forest floors, rivers flowing through building lobbies; a huge replica of a beaver dam that you crawl into only to be met by tacky fifties furniture, fake wood panelling and brightly lit, black velvet paintings of Elvis Presley. The problem is, it's difficult for me to either concentrate or appreciate with one eye on the door and the other checking for an escape route. I figure I'll warm up, chow down, use the loo and skedaddle. The guy behind the bar asks if I want a drink. They're selling beer or wine for three bucks a pop and I go, sure, give me a red wine. Four musicians start to play from a stairway landing. Something ambient; environmental. They're using makeshift instruments – sticks, metal tubes, glass jars filled with varying levels of water. A woman chants while some guy does a sort of native Indian grunting sound. A bit New Age for me. I count out coins for another wine. A body squeezes next to me.

"What do you think of this, eh?" He's talking to me. He's maybe a few years older than me, late forties, early fifties. His hands are rough, there's grime under his nails and embedded in his skin. He's wearing a baseball cap, work clothes, worn sneakers and has a tool belt strapped around his waist. "Doesn't do anything for me, personally, but I don't mind it. Gives me a laugh. Last time all it was was a pile of dirt in the middle of the floor with a circle of rocks around it. Someone's idea of art, I guess. Un-fucking-believable. Waste of time and money. But I say, what the hell? These days, someone could take a shit, stick an American flag in it, light it on fire, and call it art, right? No one bats an eye. Call it: Death of Imperialism, or whatever. So long as I don't have to clean the mess. Do you agree? Or do you disagree?"

"I never saw it," I say. "I really don't have an opinion."

"It was a pile of dirt with rocks around it. I told you."

"Yeah," I say, and finish my drink.

"Uh-huh. I catch all the shows in this block. Like I say, gives me a laugh. Plus, there's usually cheap booze. Even free sometimes. My name's Marvin. Don't worry, you don't have to shake my hand. In fact, I prefer that you don't. Fucking SARS, fucking AIDS. You can't wave goodbye to anyone these days without you're afraid your fucking arm's gonna drop off. I'm the custodian around here. I was just now repairing a toilet downstairs. Broken handle. Fuck. You'd think even one of these fairies could fix something that simple, but no, I gotta drag myself away from the TV and have it working for their little fete."

"You own the building?" I say this more as conversation than anything else.

"No fucking way. I don't own anything, brother. It's better that way. People figure when they own something, they control it. But it's the other way around, it controls you. You can't make a move without thinking about *what's-gonna-happen-if*, y'know? Me? I do what I want when I want. If I want to pack up and fucking leave, then I leave. If I tell them the toilet has to wait until tomorrow or the day after tomorrow, that's the way it is. I only came down tonight 'cause the old lady was bitchin' about somethin' and I figured I could catch a few cold ones before headin' on back. You get my drift? I'm a free fucking agent. My girlfriend, my kids, that's different. I got kids from two previous relations that I'm still payin' for. That's family and family takes priority. To a point. I take care of them; I provide for them. If I bugger off for a few days or a few weeks or even forever, they're provided for. That's what counts. I don't shirk my responsibilities when it comes to family. Anything else is a different fucking story, capiche? You want another drink?"

I instinctively pat my hands on my pants' pockets and shake my head.

"Did I ask if you had money? Did I? No. I asked if you wanted another drink. I'm buying. Your money's no good here, even if you had some." He taps the bar for two more drinks. "You're some kind of artist, am I right? Not a painter. There's no pigment on your hands; no turpentine smell."

"I'm a writer."

"A writer. Yeah. Makes sense. Soft hands. Dreamy look about you. Intellectual type. Observant. I can always tell the artists. They come to these things, schmooze, fill up on cheese and vegetables, bitch if they have to pay for a drink. They never buy anything. They don't have any fucking money 'cause they don't have any fucking real jobs. The people who actually buy art don't come to the openings. They don't want to be seen or known. They slip in when the artists' backs are turned; they send in agents; they surf the Net. All orders are done by telephone or over the computer or through a middleman. They're allergic to artists. It's not just the smells, it's the whole bullshit mewling attitude; the kowtowing, the begging, the ass-kissing that goes on. It gives them the creeps. They want this from their employees, not from people who are supposed to be fucking geniuses."

"Uh-huh. What about you? Why do you hang around if you find it all so disgusting?"

"I'm not talking about me, am I? I'm not a buyer. I fix the fucking toilet. I unclog the pipes, I repair the drywall. I've got no involvement. I'm clean. I told you, the whole jerk-off thing gives me a laugh. And the beer's cheap." He drinks. His cellphone rings. He flips it open and checks the number on the screen. "It's the girlfriend. I promised to throw a fuck into her tonight and she wants to make sure I'm not down here getting wasted."

He laughs.

"Yeah, what do you want? Uh-huh." He winks at me, like, *I told you so.* "I'll be there soon. The problem was bigger than I thought. Plugged up to the nuts. Someone had taken a crap and it wouldn't budge. I practically had to dynamite the bastard. Anyhow, now I'm having a beer with a pal. Yeah, you don't know him and no, he doesn't have long blonde hair and big tits." He smiles and mouths two words at me: *jealous cunt.* "Soon, OK, don't worry. You clean yourself up. I'm not going down on you if you're smelling like last week's snapper, ha ha. And floss. When I left you had chunks of bread between your teeth the size of golf balls. Don't worry, he's not listening. I'm turned away. Soon, I said. Soon is soon. When I get there. You're gonna be like that I'm gonna hang up. I'm gonna hang up. You hear me? I'm hanging up. I'm..." He smacks the machine shut. "Fuck you. Women, right?" he says to me. "Can't live with 'em, can't fucking kill 'em."

He taps for two more drinks.

"Listen, I really gotta be leaving."

"What's your hurry? You just got here."

"Yeah, it's just..."

"Someone's after you." He grins.

"Sorry?"

"You keep looking over your shoulder. Not like expecting a girlfriend or a buddy. More like the devil himself might walk in and tap you on the back. Am I right?"

"More or less."

"Uh-huh. What do you plan to do? Keep running? 'Cause that's what you're doing, right? Running scared? Like the old Roy Orbison tune."

He starts to sing real low, bastardizing the lyrics. Or maybe he didn't know.

"Just running scared, no place to go."

"I'm going to use the can, then I'm outta here, OK?"

"No," he says, very serious. "I mean it. What are you gonna do? 'Cause maybe I can help."

"In what way?"

"What I do for a living is repair things, yes? Anything, you name it: toilets, cracks in walls, small appliances, major appliances, computers, whatever...OK?" He nods and I nod in reply. "That's what I do to make money; to earn a living. But what I am, my true calling, is a survivalist." He gives it a second for his words to resonate. "Not like the show *Survivor* on TV, which is scripted bullshit, but the real thing. Do you understand what I'm telling you?"

"No, not really."

"Let me put it to you this way: I've staked out a piece of wasteland in northern Ontario. It's so remote, you can't drive in, you can't boat in, you can't fly in, you have to hike in. I've built myself this big motherfucker cabin in the side of a hill with my own two hands using materials I've either found there or which I've hauled in on my back. A stream provides fresh water, I've dug an outhouse, I use candles for light and cook in the fireplace for the most part, although there's propane and batteries for emergencies. In the summer I grow vegetables and can them. I catch my own game, skin it to make clothing and blankets, dry the meat and store it. There's fish in the stream. I'm an expert with knives. While I make my own traps, rods, bows and arrows, I have a cache of firearms, ammunition and explosives for dealing with any situation that might arise, be it animal or human. I can kill a person three dozen different ways with my bare hands."

"Uh-huh. And what's the purpose of all this?"

"The purpose is to be a man. The purpose is to be able to provide for my family when the shit hits the fan. The purpose is for the strong to survive while the weak perish."

"I see. You sound pretty positive that some event or catastrophe is set to happen."

"I am positive. I even know the date – September 9, 2009."

"The ninth day of the ninth month of the ninth year – 999 – the sign of the devil. Is this one of those Nostradamus predictions?"

"Fuck Nostradamus. This comes straight from the source."

"Didn't the *X-Files* have a program dealing with this date? Something about aliens and an apocalypse?"

"Yeah. And where do you think they got it?" he asks. I shrug. "The source, my friend, the source. One of the writers for the show is a survivalist. This was his way of spreading the word. You saw it and ignored it. Along with millions of others. Meanwhile, the few of us who have been chosen are preparing for the time when all hell breaks loose."

"But how did he know? I mean, what's the source?"

"The source is the source. That's all of it. There's no more. You either get it or you don't. You either learn to survive or you die."

The source is the source. Sounds like when someone asked Louis Armstrong what jazz was and he said something like "Man, if you have to ask, you'll never know." And why not the second day of the second month of 2222 or some such faraway? Why?

Because for doomsayers, a date has to be within reach (though not too close for nothing to be done), otherwise, where's the fun?

"There's still a chance for you, but you have to move quick. You have an opportunity, an open window. Someone's after you. Take care of the situation."

"Take care of the situation, how?"

"Go underground, into the sewers, learn to live like a rat. Remake yourself from the bottom up. Shave your head, shave your beard, chuck your wallet, your watch, your rings, burn your clothes, sandpaper your fingerprints, hunch over, walk with a limp – though not too much – keep it subtle, and don't fake it. Put a small stone in your shoe, that'll make it easy. You want to scar your face, tattoo your hands with a ballpoint? Go for it. Grease down your body. Learn to drink gasoline. Toughen up. Scavenge from other people's garbage. Kill a dog, rip it apart with your teeth, drink its blood and eat its heart. Chew the flesh raw. Snap the bones and suck out the marrow. Piss on the front steps of City Hall, shit on the lawn, wipe your ass with a fucking maple leaf. Speak in code. Develop your own secret language."

Shades of Kevin Spacey and *The Usual Suspects*, I think. Is this guy for real or what? Develop your own secret language? Why go to the trouble when it's easier to be like everyone else, either speaking in quotes, sampling, or appropriating wholesale from movies and television: budda-bing, budda-boom.

"When you're ready, resurface, hunt the bastards down. Give them a taste of their own medicine. Prove to them they can't screw with you. Fuck them up the ass."

"You mean...with my bare hands? Take care of them?"

"It's preferable."

"I'm not sure I'm capable of all that."

Marvin snorts. "Yeah, figures. You're like everyone else, you want things done the easy way. Or someone else to do it for you.

Except there ain't no one else, right? You're on your own."

I nod.

"Still, I'd like to help you. It's the way I'm built. The underdog." He guzzles his beer, whips a magazine from his back pocket, slaps it across to me. It's folded open to a particular page. "Read this," he whispers. "Think it over. It's your choice. Run or fight. Be a pussy or be a man." He rises from his stool, hitches his pants and turns away.

"Uh, Marvin," I stutter. "Were you going to leave some money for the drinks?"

"I don't pay," he says. "I'm the fucking custodian. They want me to pay, they can suck my cock." He gives the guy behind the bar the one finger salute and vanishes. The guy ambles toward me, his mouth twisted into a pout.

"He stiffed you?" he says. I go to explain, but he stops me. "Don't worry, you're not the first. Marvin's always pushing some story or another onto someone then splitting the scene without paying."

"Do you ever go after him?"

"Oh, if he wants to play the big shot, let him. So long as he comes to fix the toilet when I call him."

"Yeah, the point is, I'm kind of short on cash at the moment."

"We're all short on cash, honey. That's a given. But never fear. Anyone who puts up with Marvin, so that I don't have to, deserves a couple of drinks on the house." He tops up my glass. "Chin-chin," he says.

"Cheers," I say. I lock my eyes on the newsprint Marvin handed to me. In bold letters it reads: THE TIME HAS COME TO DEFEND YOURSELF! Then less obtrusively (though only just): **Fight back against attackers! Don't be a victim! Feel completely safe! NOW you no longer need to live in fear of muggers, rapists, burglars! No federal licence or gun permits needed!**

Exclamation points, capital letters and bold type abound as I attempt to recall the latest stats on violent crime in North America. As usual, my memory is faulty, though not that faulty, and my sense is that over the past ten years the incidence of violent crime in major cities has, in fact, dropped twelve per cent, whereas in the mediums of television, film, magazines, the portrayal of violent crime has risen by over six hundred per cent. You do the math and go figure. I read on.

That's right! Feel completely safe and secure wherever you go. Yes! In just seconds you can immediately disable any attacker. Because you are now armed with the most effective .22-caliber non-lethal tear-gas handguns ever devised. Just imagine what this could mean to you and your loved ones. Both guns will fire a sudden burst that will instantly disable any attacker. Each shot sounds so real that the intruder will be easily scared away – and well he should be! But the best part is that you do not need a federal firearms licence to own or carry these personal protective weapons. These weapons are not applicable to the Brady Bill. So now you can walk without fear.

Tear-gas handgun? It all sounds very bizarre and at the same time very cool and inviting. Which is, I guess, the point. What else?

Solid metal! Dependable products of master European gunsmiths. Order now! These desirable, high-quality guns are beautifully balanced. Our revolver is the famous Snub Nose model 8-shot side-loading cylinder. Our 6-shot heavy duty frame, semi-automatic is clip fed. Both guns respond perfectly to your every movement and are extremely easy to handle. So don't take crime lying down. Fight back and win! Both the automatic and revolver can be loaded with either tear gas cartridges or blanks and not standard ammunition. As you can see, these handsome, solid metal guns will fit easily into a pocket, purse or in our specially designed gun holster. These precision-made guns are extremely sturdy yet lightweight. They can literally save your life in time of need. So act today! **Your choice NOW only $29.95. Why pay $79.95?** Why indeed? I check out the order form.

Yes! I want instant protection. I am 18 years of age or over. I have enclosed my cheque, cash or money order. I understand that these guns should not be used to commit a crime or inflict pain upon innocent people. Sorry, no COD. It all sounds too incredible, yes? But wait, there's more. *SATISFACTION GUARANTEED OR YOUR MONEY BACK. Just return your gun. No questions asked. We will refund your money. Both guns are unconditionally guaranteed for 30 days.* Well...you'd have to be a fool, right? I flip the page.

BLANK PHOTO ID CARDS. Make laminated photo IDs on any typewriter.

SONIC SUPER EAR. Hear a whisper, bird call or concert up to 100 feet away. THIS is NOT a TOY or GADGET. Similar style used by Detectives, Surveillance Experts, Now Available for Private Use! Comes complete with high performance adjustable, padded stereo headphones.

AUTHORS WANTED! Leading subsidy book publisher seeks manuscripts of all types: fiction, non-fiction, poetry, scholarly, juvenile and religious works, etc. YOU TOO CAN BECOME A PUBLISHED WRITER!

I can't help but smile. It's funny, yet it's not funny. People are buying this: hook, line and liar. I raise my head and – what's this? The guy serving drinks is huddled over the telephone, cocking an eye in my direction. Dangled around his neck I spy a small set of headphones and with his free hand he's toying with what appears to be a Sonic Super Ear. Shit! I drop the magazine to the floor and break for the exit. A cop car speeding my way, siren off, lights flashing. I keep to the shadows and head west, young man.

A quick glance over the shoulder spots two cops jumping

from the squad car, revolvers in hand. My guess is that they're not the tear-gas handgun variety either, but the real McCoy. Someone's getting fucking serious and can everyone be in on this or is it mere coincidence and a B and E in progress or *Murder in the Cathedral* or domestic dispute – Marvin's main squeeze cold-cocking him with a fry pan for passing out drunk in front of the boob tube without having performed his husbandly duty – or false alarm or maybe a performance piece and part of the art show? Not bloody likely. The cops rush into the gallery. I zip up a side street and figure to wind my way into Parkdale where I can maybe lose myself in a gutted warehouse or broken-down factory or vacant garage or salvage yard or something.

Meanwhile, I never had time to use the john and I've got to take a crap. "Take a crap?" What did George Carlin say? We don't *take* a crap, we *leave* a crap. Right, ha ha. The question is: where? The cops will be in *hot pursuit* (as the voice-over says in those old flicks), with APBs and German shepherds and helicopters with searchlights and megaphones and undercover fuzz and paid informant rat finks and cavalry and Indian scouts and Boy Scouts and little old ladies with knitting needles and cans of mace and whatever else official or unofficial muscle in order to track me like a lowdown mangy dog and feed me to the wolves. How take the necessary time to drop my pants and void my bowels?

Like there's a choice.

I scoot up a lane and park myself between a section of fence and a garage where I spot a flyer for Future Shop flapping in a grey bin. Finally, I mumble, one of these will have some real practical use. I crumple a page, unbuckle and assume the position. Naturally, whether due to fear or embarrassment or *who knows what*, things do not proceed as smoothly or as rapidly as I might have hoped and I strain and relax, relax and strain, as the fecal matter inches its way slowly from my nether regions. At least the rain has stopped, I think, there's no traffic and I'm in relative darkness. Still, isn't this the first sort of place the cops would investigate? While I ponder this and other inevitabilities, I recall a passage from Graeme Gibson's novel, *Communion*.

Leaving by the side door, into the alley, it's dark, he's wearing running shoes and goes directly to the park, then into the ravine, he moves with empty grace, through underbrush, a path beside the road because sometimes there are others... At night, when there's no longer the noise of traffic on Yonge Street, with winos sleeping heavily in the bushes, he emerges from the ravine, he must eat and knows which houses are likely to be open and where there are no dogs. He's motionless by the catalpa, he's watching, listening, then he vaults the fence and moves quickly to the back door and slips inside. He's selective by instinct and rather than have them miss anything, begin to watch for him, he'll visit three or four houses, taking a little from each. He drinks from the milk bottle, there's cold meat in a drawer beneath the freezer, he takes some fruit, several slices of bread, he puts it all in his pockets, picks up a tomato, takes another mouthful of milk and starts for the back door...

Kind of spooky and slightly unnerving if you're a homeowner. Lucky bastard main character Fripp though, who can behave in this manner without fear and no sense of guilt or remorse and no thought of reprisals or repercussions, whereas I am confounded by all such social affectations, causing me to judge every action.

As here, now, the embarrassment of taking a crap (though a natural bodily function) in public; the shame attached, worried that some poor unfortunate might inadvertently step and soil a shoe in my droppings.

Even as I wipe with the crumpled flyer, I consider the damage that might be caused by the cancerous dyes attaching to my anus. This thought is immediately followed by the possibility that science might be able to identify and trace me via my spoor.

The newspapers would have a field day.

What would my mother think?

Then, to enter somebody's sacred home and steal something? Even a tomato? I couldn't do it. Though, perhaps out of necessity; balls to the wall and the base desire to survive: sack, pillage, rape, maim, kill…?

Naw, I don't think so. I mean, I even remembered to place extra sheets of the flyer on the ground beneath me so that I am better able to clean up my mess and toss it into the garbage can. The remainder of the flyer I fold in neat quarters and politely, civic-mindedly, pitch back into the grey box.

Catalpa, I go, hitching my pants. Why is it always *catalpa* trees in novels? What the hell is a *catalpa* tree, anyway? Why not a maple or an oak, which I can't distinguish, one from the other, either, but at least have some faint notion?

I carry this thought of catalpa trees with me as I pad my way west, the thought gradually giving way to an idea, then to an image, whether correct or no: catalpa trees looming both sides of the street, catalpa leaves beneath my feet to cushion the sound, a swirl of catalpa leaves above and around me to shield me from view. I am silent and invisible; a ghost in search of some safe retreat, some comfortable haunt.

Corny, yes, but it beats the alternative – that I'm running under street lamps with a glow-in-the-dark bull's eye painted on my back and a time bomb ticking up my ass.

8

Advocatus diabolo: Devil's advocate

Seven nights spent in back of a scrap yard, sleeping stretched out within two rusted oil drums, hollowed out and snugged together at the ends, the joint protected by a ragged piece of heavy-duty plastic drop cloth wrapped around and weighted at the sides with bricks. Pretty ingenious, considering I'm no survivalist, and not bad, really, as I managed to line the drums with a discarded futon and cover myself with a couple of blankets gleaned from beside the Salvation Army drop-off bin. Not exactly stealing as they were sitting there for anyone to find and utilize for their own purpose.

Money's gone, naturally, vanished the first three days on a ration of fast food and cups of coffee in doughnut shops, which also served as great spots to keep warm and use the keyed washrooms. Stone broke, that small luxury is kaput and now it's in and out of stores and buildings through the day and into the evening for a bit of warmth and toilet time. Or prowling the halls and facilities of St. Joseph's Health Centre, which had been a bonus, initially. Given its size and maze-like interior, it was easy to avoid detection. I was able to give myself a good scrub, and wash my single pair of underwear, though clothes, hair and beard were getting rattier and everyone began to recognize me, gave me the evil eye, prodded me with questions as to my business in the place, more often ordered me to vacate the premises and it's obvious that my visitation privileges are coming to a prompt and unhappy end.

The local library was a place of refuge for a time, but, again, due to my off-putting appearance and increasing disagreeable body odour I've been requested never to return upon pain of horsewhipping. Or worse. An attempt to show my library card to sort of validate my existence as a responsible citizen proved fatal, as the woman at the desk – by all appearances, a meek and mousy type – snatched the card from my fingers, tore it to small pieces in front of me, told me that not only was the card invalid, it was fraudulent and threatened to phone the authorities. Whoever *they* were, she wasn't specific.

I vamoosed.

In a similar vein, attempts to call my family collect in Vancouver each time met with a recorded voice message saying, *We're sorry, but that number is not in service.*

Liars!

I am cut off from all and sundry.

Bottom line – there is no room at the inn for this vagrant soul and it's simply a matter of time before I'm discovered and wrested from my rough nest in the scrap yard as well. The real question is: why has it taken them this long? Why have I been allowed to roam freely this past week? Why? Because they know there's nowhere for me to go and nothing for me to do except sit back and watch as the bottom falls out of my world totally, completely and irreversibly.

Worse, I've become oblivious to my own rank smell, which can't be a good sign.

Oh, where are the catalpa trees of yesteryear? Oh, where are
they now?

Gone the way of the dodo bird, it seems, along with every
other star-struck romantic.

I wake in a sweat, having been dreaming female flesh of no fixed
identity, simply breasts, mouths, vaginas, buttocks clambering
around my still stiff cock. I work the erection with my hand a
bit, but whether weak from lack of food, too tired, unable to
fully concentrate, or overall feeling of pitiful self-disgust (given
my overall sad and pathetic condition and that of my immediate
surroundings), the joint balks and shrinks. Perhaps after a nice
hot shower, with a few candles, a glass of red wine and a copy of
this month's *Playboy* magazine...

Right.

It's mild tonight, with a clear sky, full moon and barely a
breeze to shudder the tree branches. A fat mama raccoon shuffles
along the fence top with four little ones in tow. Bats slash across
the stars. Cats prowl. Rats scrabble about and I recall reading
stories of babies having their fingers and toes nibbled off by
the vile creatures while they slept soundly in their cribs. What
else about rats? Yes, of course, there's the always memorable
Black Death or bubonic plague, and leaving a sinking ship,
and that movie, *Willard*. Very pleasant Edgar Allan Poe-type
thoughts and I must remember to always count my digits in the
morning.

Rats live on no evil star. A palindrome, as well as the phrase
poet Anne Sexton wanted engraved on her tombstone. For
what reason? To what end?

Here and there across the yard, the glint of green rats' eyes
flicker in the moonlight.

I pose the question: will I be able to hold out until spring
and the weather turns warmer? Today at a fruit stand I picked up
an apple, rolled it around in my hand, sniffed it and considered

walking off with it. I figured, who's going to miss one lousy apple? Then my mother's voice entered my head, saying: what if everyone thought that way and took one lousy apple? What if everyone who visited the Grand Canyon decided to throw a rock into it? Soon there'd be no Grand Canyon, just a crevice full of rocks; soon, the grocer would be out of business and unable to support his family.

Yeah, yeah, Mom, I know, and you're right, but I'm hungry.

How long before apples grow on the trees? In summer, I seem to recall, there are apples all over the city. No one touches them. They fall to the ground, get booted about by kids, stepped on, swept away, and are eventually gathered up and trucked off by the city to be turned into compost. Small, gnarly, brown apples, to be sure. Even so, they must be edible. It would be a start. If I could get my hands on some seed packets, I could grow my own small garden. There's a plot of earth in back of me, between the building and the fence. How difficult could it be? Plant potatoes, green beans, zucchini, carrots, corn and pumpkins. Simply dig a furrow in the ground, drop in the seeds, cover with earth, add water, watch them take shape, harvest and eat. Easy. Maybe I could even find some way to can or preserve them to get me through the winter. A real Walden Pond type of thing. Not quite a survivalist, maybe, in Marvin's terms, though at least self-sufficient. Maybe a few chickens for eggs and...

OK, stop right now! This is crazy talk, plain and simple. What's that phrase? *Quem Deus vult perdere, prius dementat: those whom God wishes to destroy, he first makes mad.* Bingo! This isn't Walden Pond and I'm sure as hell not Henry David Thoreau. Besides, doesn't the story go that while he was writing about surviving on his own in nature, his mother would arrive by train each day to bring him a boxed lunch? And in the evenings he'd hop across the pond to Ralph Waldo Emerson's house, sit on the porch, talk philosophy, nibble on cakes and drink mint juleps? And after the first quiet snowfall didn't he promptly pack up and scurry back home to his warm, roaring fireplace and comfy featherbed?

In the meantime, up river, the Thoreau family business – a pencil factory, if you can believe the irony – was chugging away, set to make even more of a mockery of Henry's *return to the land* sham by eventually dumping enough effluent in the river to transform Walden Pond, for a time, into the most polluted body of water in the country.

Whatever. I drift asleep, jolt up a few hours later with the frantic sense that something is nibbling at my ears. I bat away furiously with my hands, hitting nothing but air. Then I hear a voice and I freeze. I rub my eyes and make out a shadowy shape hunched over and leaned against the building, barely visible in the moonlight. The voice emanates from that shape. It's a woman's voice. She's speaking to me but I can't make out more than a couple of words here and there. The rest is gibberish. She approaches me and drops to her knees. I recognize her. It's Eileen, from Friends of the Ecology, whose unofficial wake I attended.

That's it, I think, I have gone mad. Worse (and for whatever no good reason), my erection has returned, more raging than ever.

Eileen continues to speak, and as she does, I'm able to decipher the better part of what she's saying. I recognize that the words are English, but the spelling is jumbled, the larger words at any rate, with most of the individual letters spoken phonetically.

Wasn't there some research project done through the University of Cambridge or similar bigwig institution somewhere in the US that said as long as the first and last letters of a word were in the correct position then it didn't matter what the rest of the order was? It could be a total mess, yet the human mind could easily manage to make sense of it?

"Eileen, is that really you?"

"Yes, Votcir. It's rlaely me. Dno't be ariafd. I need to tlak to you. I msut tlel you smohtenig, smohtenig trilerbe."

Bats keen, cats yowl, rats scrabble, raccoons (backlit by the moon) rise up on their hind legs like ghouls as I attempt to concentrate on Eileen's words, made further difficult by the achy fact of the aforementioned, unwanted erection.

"I thought you died?"

"My bdoy deid, but my sripit cnutinoes to raom the etarh," she shudders.

Shades of Charles Dickens and *A Christmas Carol*.

"What do you want to tell me."

"Bwerae, Votcir! Tehy mrudreed me and tehy wlil mdruer you too."

"Murdered you? I heard you died of a brain tumour?"

"No Votcir," she wails. "It was mdruer, mdruer msot fuol! Unop my srecue huor tehy cmae and puroed teihr vlie pisoin itno my ear!"

Christ, now she's dipped into *Hamlet*. What have I got myself into? At the closing curtain: murder, ghosts, madness, suicide, treachery, bloodshed and a stage full of dead bodies, including yours truly?

"Who murdered you Eileen? Why?"

"Tehy! Tehm! The pwores that be! The nmruelsebs oens! The flescelas oens! Toshe taht wulod rlue by froce! Tehy wenatd to suht me up; to keep me form dniscrevoig the tutrh and tlenilg the wlord."

"Yeah, but who are they? Can you be more specific?"

"It is a cirspnocay wcihh has estixed for etrentiy and wcihh ctniuones to evlvoe! Letsin to me Voctir, I hevna't mcuh tmie. You msut mkae a cohcie."

"Choice? What sort of choice?"

"You are at a csordasros and you msut cohose weethhr to cnotnuie fwarord or to take a drefenift ptah."

Oh, here we go again with the mumbo-jumbo. A crossroads,

a bridge – it's like talking with my ex-wife. The next thing you know she'll break out the Tarot cards and flip through the deck: The King of Swords, a warning. The Queen of Pentacles, a good sign; a sign of hope. The Wheel, obvious. The Twins, a false clue. The Fool, here, denotes a change. The Hanged Man, not to be mistaken for tragedy, merely some necessity.

Can't anyone give a straight answer anymore?

"Ooooooh," she wails, and the hairs on my neck stand on end. "The sun will rsie soon and I msut be gnoe. Ufturntolenay, I conant tlel you mroe tahn tihs. It is not wnihtin my pewor. All I can say is taht, touhgh all ptahs are the smae, all ptahs are derneffit; wilhe all ptahs laed to dtaeh, it is how we lvie taht's iptromnat. Rmebmeer me! Rmebmeer me!"

Eileen pushes to her feet, stumbles off and disappears into the darkness. The bats, cats, rats and raccoons give a final wild flurry and settle back into their normal nightly routine.

All paths lead to death. That's cheery. *Not how we die, but how we live is important.* Thank you for that, Eileen. But which path? I mean, I have no idea which path I'm on now, never mind what the alternatives are. I fondle my erection and think, the smart path to follow at this moment is the one that gets me laid. Ha, fat chance. I give a couple of tight strokes and, sure enough, the damn joint withers. So much for that. What's the term they use nowadays? Not *masturbation*, which I reckon has the smack of Christian guilt attached, but *self-pleasuring*, the act placed in the same category as reading a good potboiler or watching a favourite TV sitcom: *Excuse me honey, I'm just going to go into the living room for a while and wank off. That's fine dear, but don't make a mess. I just had the upholstery cleaned yesterday.*

Or in the middle of a business meeting, saying: *Pardon me.* Whip it out, lay it on the table and jerk off into a water bottle. Or a pair of crotchless panties. *Just be a minute. Hope you don't mind.* Tip the little man in the canoe to ecstasy with a well-practiced fingertip.

Ah, that's better!

The story of Cleopatra who had her own special footwear specially designed with horns on the back of the heels so she could sit with a foot beneath her crotch and rock her way blissfully through boring political discussions: Bring me the head of John the Baptist! she moans. Or Julius Caesar or Marc Antony or Attila the Hun for that matter.

No big deal. Just a bit of self-pleasuring.

Swell. Though, no self-pleasuring for this guy. Oh no, things have taken a complete one-eighty and it's fucking downhill from here on in.

All paths lead to death.

Okey-dokey, Eileen. Yes, thanks for that. Thanks for dropping by. Maybe come see me again when you've got more time. We'll chew the fat. Shoot the shit. Play another little game of *Stump the Poor Asshole Poet.*

I yawn, crawl under the blankets, close my eyes, sigh a deep sigh. I figure after this rough night, I'll conk right out and, in fact, I feel myself start to doze. Simultaneously and in total sync, I get another raging hard-on! Sonofabitch! What do you want from me? I try to do something with you, help you out, and you won't have any part. Are you playing with me or what? The phrase *gone to seed* comes to mind wherein the dying plant makes with its final burst, or the cockroach, panicked by the shadow of the folded newspaper, ejaculates its egg pod for a desperate shot at extending the species and is this what's going on here? My body pumped with the fear of death, seeking one last hurrah? Perhaps. I grab with both hands and it's like I'm a character from a Beardsley print straight out of Lysistrata. It's like I'm holding onto a goddamned tree trunk. I want to orgasm, I'd like to orgasm, I need to orgasm, it would be good and healthy to orgasm, but I'm too tired, too tired.

I dream the boardroom scene. I dream the woman with the crotchless panties. I dream her fiddling with herself, parting her labia, penetrating her vagina with her finger, stirring up the juices, puddling the tan leather upholstery, toying with her clitoris, urging herself to orgasm. I dream being in the room after she's gone, getting down on my knees in front of her chair, sniffing the moist seat. I dream unzipping my cock and ejaculating onto her dampness. Unlike my recent failed attempts while awake, in the dream, all proceeds swimmingly and I witness the spurt of fine white come mingle with the woman's juices. The pool appears to foam for a second, then begins to swirl and eddy. My eye is drawn into the vortex and, from within, I see a hideous, pained face writhing from the mix. It crawls forward, dragging a monstrous body along with it. I fall onto my back, scuttle across the floor into a corner of the room, my limp dick hanging ridiculous through my fly, like a tongue of useless fabric one is meant to scissor and discard.

The great hairy thing looms over me, making hissing, gargling noises. Its shape changes constantly so that it resembles first human then beast, then combinations thereof, then neither human nor beast. It appears to want to communicate something to me, but I don't understand. I'm too much afraid and there's too much going on within the creature itself. The more it tries, the more I shake my head *no* and the more frustrated and angry it gets. Finally, it rears back, steadies itself, struggles to control itself, forces its mouth painfully into a sort of rough oval, the black tongue working its way toward the yellowed teeth, a guttural sound rising from the throbbing chest, into the throat, and I catch a single word slur through its quavering lips.

"Lucian," it hacks.

Then struggle a second time, and, "Luciano," it spits and, defeated, sinks screaming into the mucked leather.

Holy fuck, I think, still whaling away at my pecker. What is happening? What is going on, fer Chrissakes? Where is the fucking God in the fucking machine that is supposed to step in and straighten out this fucking mess?

I had to ask.

The crunch of automobile tires motoring across gravel and an abrupt screeching halt outside my makeshift home stops me cold. Dawn has not yet struck and I peek outside the blankets straight into a pair of headlights. The rear passenger door slowly opens. The unmistakable form of a high heel attached to a woman's trim ankle emerges. Next, the woman herself strides forward and situates herself within the glare of headlights, somewhere midway between me and the car. Her outline remains relatively unfocused to my eyes as she shifts her weight from foot to foot, though I can see that she has strong, firm legs, an angular frame, is about five foot six inches tall with shoulder length reddish-brown hair, wears a dark, business-like short skirt and jacket, has an overcoat draped over one arm and clenches a briefcase in the hand of that same arm. With her other hand, she flips a Zippo and lights what appears to be a rum-dipped, wine-tipped Colt cigar. She blows the smoke into a blue cloud in front of her face and over her head. I can hear the engine idle behind her as if in harmony with her own measured breathing and heart rate.

"Victor Stone," she says.

I want to fire back: *who wants to know*? but her words have not been delivered as a question or even as a statement. They've been delivered as a simple hard fact, so I bury the impulse.

Yes, I nod.

"Come with me."

There's no fighting it. I've already tossed the blankets aside and am halfway to my feet.

"Who are you?"

"That's irrelevant."

"Come with you where?"

"Does it matter?"

I shrug. Earlier visions of concrete booties, bullet holes, knife wounds, blows to the head with a hard, blunt object and bodies ending at the bottoms of rivers, sides of dirt roads, the basements of warehouses and so on, slip into old files of bad movie memories. Up close, the woman has the face of an angel. A tough, yet strikingly beautiful angel to be sure. A femme fatale of the classic film noir style. If she's going to do me in, what the hell? Better her than the fucking black creature from the fucking black lagoon.

So, again, lead on Macduff!

"You look like shit," she says. "Put this on."

"Thanks," I say, and slip into the London Fog overcoat draped over her arm. "It fits," I smile.

"Of course it fits. What did you expect?"

I drop my hands to my sides and twist my lips.

"Get in," she says and motions me into the back seat. The vehicle is a sleek black Cadillac with a roomy rear interior. A tinted window separates the passengers from the driver. The woman taps the glass and we're into reverse. I watch my former home flicker and vanish as we wheel onto the street.

"You stink," she says and opens the window a crack. "You stink to high heaven."

I hang my head and fold my hands in my lap.

"And, you've got an erection."

"Well, yeah, sort of... It's one of those things."

"Uh-huh," she says, dragging on her Colt. "Do me a favour, don't get any ideas, OK? This is strictly business."

"Sure," I nod, and recognize there won't be a lot of small talk along the way to...wherever.

I'm correct on this score. Absolutely no small talk. None. Zip. Nada. Zero. In fact, no talk at all. The woman puffs her Colt through full, scarlet lips, drums her red painted nails on the briefcase in her lap while I stare out the window and take in the view: scenery rolling by, the sun rising steadily in the east.

We pull up in front of the lobby to the Four Seasons Hotel. The woman steps out, I follow. I try to look as inconspicuous as possible, though no one seems alarmed or surprised at my presence, my appearance. She doesn't bother checking us in. Such arrangements have obviously been taken care of ahead of time. We march straight to the elevator, she punches Penthouse and it's up, up, up to the top floor where she flips an electronic pass-key from her jacket pocket, opens the door and we enter.

"What do you think?" she says, as she places her briefcase on a coffee table and flops her curvy frame across a sofa. "What is your impression?"

"Very nice," I say, taking in the grandeur.

"Uh-huh. A sight better than your last digs."

"Yeah."

"Yeah," she mimics, and lights up another Colt. She points with the Zippo. "On the table, there, you see a box. In the box is a set of fresh clothes, including underwear, socks and shoes. Take the box through that door, into the bedroom, where you will find a bathroom. Undress, jump into the shower, or run yourself a hot bath, if you prefer. There are men's toiletries – shaving gear and such – on the sink. Scrub yourself down, clean yourself up, brush your teeth, gargle, floss – especially floss – put on the new outfit, place your old clothes in the box, leave the box on the floor in a corner somewhere, to be picked up and disposed of by the maid. In short, relax, enjoy yourself, take your time, pour yourself a drink. There's champagne chilled and opened in the ice bucket behind you, Scotch in the decanter, or you can uncork a bottle of wine. I believe you have a choice of either French or Italian. You're a red drinker, correct? Perhaps a nice Amarone? I'll be enjoying the champagne, myself."

"Shall I pour for you?" I reach for the bottle.

"No thank you." She rises, glides toward the bucket, catches my eye in the mirror. "No offence, but you're filthy and you smell like a pig. Maybe later."

"Uh-huh." I grab the decanter of Scotch along with a glass. I notice how grimy my hands are against the sparkling cut crystal. I pick up the box, snug it under my arm and shuffle into the bedroom.

I opt for the tub. There's bubble bath and sweet smelling soap and shampoo and plenty of hot water. There's a button you can press for a Jacuzzi effect, so I hit it and feel the water jet into my achy muscles and dirt-filled pores. I pour myself a drink and luxuriate. The Scotch is fabulous: smooth, fragrant and peaty tasting. The way I like it.

After two large shots, I raise myself out of the tub and dry off with a towel the size of a small island. I go to the sink, trim my beard, give myself a shave, rub moisturizing oils into my skin and splash my face down with lotions. I wipe my armpits with deodorant. I brush my teeth. There's a container of dental floss in the vanity shelf, but I choose to take a pass.

There are limits, I think.

Through it all, the sailor's still standing at attention and it takes some effort to manage a long, leisurely piss in the antiseptic white toilet bowl.

I hang a hand towel over the erection. Nothing to be done except work around it, it seems. I cut my nails and blow-dry my thinning hair. I drink more Scotch. I gargle with the stuff. It tastes funny blended with the minty toothpaste.

This is the life, I think, and swallow.

The clothes are terrific. Italian cut, right down to the underwear. Everything fits perfectly, as if they were made for me. Slacks, shirt, jacket – the shoes feel as if I've been wearing them for months, they're so comfortable. The handkerchief has my initials and is scented. These guys think of everything.

What guys?

Fuggedabouddit!

After this transformation, I have half an idea that the

woman will have slipped into something more comfortable herself, like: high heels and a birthday suit. I mean, isn't that how it goes? All this nasty attitude as mere foreplay toward the inevitable seduction scene? Wrong. Not even close. She sits fully clothed on the sofa sipping champagne, flipping through business papers. Although she does stop flipping for a brief moment to lean back and give me the once over.

"It's an improvement."

"Thanks," I say. So, who knows? Perhaps there's hope yet. "You like?" I do a spin. I'm a little drunk. She can probably tell I'm a little drunk.

"I said it's an improvement. Don't push it."

"Right," I nod. "Gotcha."

"You still have that erection."

There's a noticeable bulge in the expensive Italian pants.

"Nothing I can do. It seems to have a mind of its own."

"Uh-huh," she says, and stretches an arm sideways across her body toward the lamp.

This is it, I think, she's going to turn out the light. I feel like Pavlov's dog: my skin tingles and my mouth waters as I watch her. There's no preventing it, I'm in stimulus/response mode; conditioned reflex. She's wearing a white blouse with the top two buttons undone. Her bra is cut low and one breast swells as she leans. Her skirt hikes above her thigh.

"I can make a call," she says, and slaps her hand on the phone.

"A call?"

"To a service. We can get someone to come over. To take care of it."

"You mean, like, a prostitute?"

"An escort service. It's their job. They do these things."

"I don't think I could."

"Why not?"

"I have this – I don't know – funny – *principle* – I guess

you'd call it. I don't pay for sex. Directly. With cash. I have to believe that the woman is actually interested in having sex with me; that she finds me somewhat attractive. There has to be some sort of personal connection; some drama."

The woman straightens and adjusts her skirt.

"Personal connection and drama? That's rich. Let me tell you something, Victor. You suffer from the misconception, the illusion, the de-lusion, that you are some type of present-day Romantic figure: Keats or Shelley, say. Or Byron, complete with club foot prepared to swim the Hellespont. Which you're not. What you are is an idiot and a loser. And a conservative, middle-class idiot and loser at that. You have the misguided conception that you are a Romantic, an *artiste*, because you write *poetry*; because you have certain *ideals*; because you have *integrity*."

The woman stresses each key word, hisses, juts out her chin, twists her face, forms quotation marks in the air with her fingers. She taps out another Colt and lights up. Blue smoke spirals from her ruby lips.

"You're wrong. Dead wrong. Just as you're wrong about the Romantics. What did Freud have to say on the subject? People become artists for three reasons: wealth, fame and beautiful lovers. That's it. The single concern the Romantics had was with themselves. They fucked their friends and everyone else around them. That's what the Romantics were all about – self-pleasure. They drank, doped, screwed, whored, lied, betrayed and whined. My God, did they whine! It was all me, me, me. And the poetry and philosophy? Mere tools used to pick the pockets of the rich or get into someone's pants. Foreplay, if you will, toward the ultimate goal, that being no more than simple bodily satisfaction. There are many reasons to have sex, Victor, but in the end it's all about one thing – the physical pleasure in the act of getting off: orgasm. Are you telling me that you have no qualms about *making the scene with a magazine* or jerking off with a cored apple but you won't entertain the notion of doing it with a woman simply because she charges you a flat fee?"

"How did you know about the cored apple?"

"Never mind."

"Would you consider having sex with me?"

"Ha! Have sex with you? For what possible reason?"

"No reason. I mean, if it's just a physical act toward the pleasure of achieving an orgasm. I presume you do like to orgasm, don't you?"

"To begin with, you disgust me, both physically and as a human being in general. Secondly, I am here on business. Strictly business."

"But for many, business is pleasure and vice versa." It's the erection talking, I know, but, what the hell? I've dug myself in this far.

"For whom?"

"Prostitutes."

"Prostitutes find no pleasure in business, believe me."

"They find business in pleasure." I close in on her.

"They find business in the pleasure of others. Or pleasuring others, to be more precise."

"And is that your business?" I crouch at her knees.

"What?"

"Pleasuring others." I stare her straight in the eyes and lick my lips.

"In a manner of speaking. You're drunk, Victor, and the job of semantics is getting beyond your ken. I need to talk to you and our time here grows short. Shall I make this call or not?"

"Would you watch?"

"Watch you partake in the act of rutting? I think not."

"Then, forget it."

"Fine. Can we get down to the business at hand?"

I smile. She throws a look at me, like: don't even think about it!

"You mean there's no – not even a chance of..."

"In your dreams." she says. "Hand job or otherwise," and blows a smoke ring in my face.

"Ah." I'm getting the picture, though my erection remains unimpressed. I cough, shrug, sigh, stand. "OK. What sort of business?"

"Recently you were made a rather generous offer to join the Venture Publications family of authors, correct?"

"Correct."

"You refused that offer, correct?"

"Correct."

"I have been retained by Venture Publications to present this offer one final time."

She lays a contract on the coffee table along with a pen.

"And if I still don't want to sign?"

The woman extracts a cardboard portfolio from her briefcase, untwirls the red tie ribbon and dumps a pile of glossy black and white photographs in front of me. I push at them. They're all of me: in Chinatown, in the gallery with Marvin, running up King Street, taking a dump in the back lane, drinking coffee in the doughnut shop, holding an apple, asleep in the oil drums.

"I see. The problem is – and what I've been trying to explain to everyone – is that I don't have another novel in me, so, what's the point of signing? I mean, the bottom line is – and while I understand that Venture Publications owns my contract and I have absolutely no choice in the matter and that this is simply a formality – I am unable to provide them with the expected and necessary new work to fulfill my end of the bargain. I'm of absolutely no use to the company." I grin a broad, shit-eating grin and pour another Scotch.

Put that in your pipe and smoke it, I think. The woman doesn't so much as blink, never mind skip a beat.

"You're missing the big picture, Victor." She crushes her Colt in the ashtray. "What we own is the name *Victor Stone*. We don't give a flying fuck about you or your work. At this precise moment we have half a dozen skilled hacks developing manuscripts based on the voice and style of *Victor Stone*. We're ready to go to print with a new novel in the fall. Translation rights have been sold worldwide. A movie deal has already been inked. There are negotiations for a TV series as well as an animated video game. The *Victor Stone* ad campaign is underway and soon you'll be pushing *soup to nuts* everything from fountain pens to watches to hemorrhoid creams to American Express cards. Do you understand me? Am I being clear?"

"If that's true, why do you need me?"

"It's always better to have a face connected to the name, Victor. Makes it more personal for the buying public. Of course, if you decide to refuse our offer, we will simply create a myth around you – that of the eccentric recluse, let's say. The problem with this is, there can only be so many *eccentric recluses* in the world before the novelty wears thin and the public's interest wanes and eventually disappears altogether. Our research indicates that, in your case, we should be good for at least three to five years. Not much, but better than nothing."

"You've bought my identity."

"Exactly."

I knock back my Scotch and consider.

"I could start again; write under a new name," I pose.

"You could – except that whatever you chose to write would always appear as a second-rate imitation of *Victor Stone*." The woman continues to stab the air with quotation marks, as if to irritate me. "So, unlikely that anyone would publish you. Besides, how old are you now?"

"Forty-five."

"And how long were you slaving away: writing, rewriting, submitting to magazines, frequenting readings, meeting editors, not to mention working shitty jobs to finance your *habit* and whatnot, before someone finally published your first book?"

"About twenty years."

The woman purses her lips, smiles, nods, taps the end of a Colt against the package.

"Why me?" I ask.

"Why you, what?" A flame jumps from her hand.

"Why was I chosen?"

"Luck of the draw. Nothing more. It could've been one of thousands of would-be writers. Though we don't deal simply with writers. Our stable includes every celebrity-type vocation. You believe you're alone? You believe you're special? That you're the only one? You're not. We have family wherever the limelight strikes. Take a peek at this." She selects a sheet of paper from a folder. "The list is selective. It's meant to provide you with names we thought you'd recognize; be familiar with."

I lean in and do a quick scan. It's incredible. The list contains some of the top names in literature, art, sports, movies, politics, science, business, television.

"These are all members of the Venture Publications family?"

"They are all members of the *family*, yes, though not necessarily attached specifically to Venture Publications, as this is merely a small subsidiary branch of a much larger conglomerate, which, again, is merely a small branch of something larger, and so on and so on."

"I see. Behind the door is a guard and behind a second door is a much larger and more powerful guard."

"Don't go getting all literary on me, Victor. Franz Kafka was a coup for our organization and only too unfortunate for us that he died at such an early age."

Ohmygod, I think. "Franz Kafka," and I make with the quotation marks inside my head.

"The company has also decided to make one slight concession in your contract." The woman wriggles straight back in the sofa, crosses one leg over the other and tugs at an upper button on her blouse.

It's the first time I've seen her show any sign of discomfort;

as if it's personal. What have they commissioned her to offer; what *slight* concession? The one-eyed trouser snake raises its ugly head; rubs against the silk underwear; twitches.

Maybe there's hope yet?

"Venture Publications agrees to print one book of *poems* during your five year term with us." She spits the word *poems* as if it's cut into her lips, then fumbles a quick pull on her Colt by way of cauterizing the wound.

"Poems?" The word has a not dissimilar effect on me as the twitch in my pants immediately subsides.

"Yes. I was against it, personally, but..." She knocks a bit of ash onto the carpet. "That's the deal. Take it or leave it. Choose either this." She gestures broadly with the Colt, a blue plume of smoke trailing, to the suite and everything in it. "Or this." She points the toe of her high heel to the stack of photos.

"Yeah. I guess I'd have to be crazy, right?" I pick up the pen and begin to sign where indicated.

"Take heart, Victor. With your new-found prestige and wealth, you can ease your conscience by taking up a cause. Others before have done the same. Save the whales, feed the children, help develop a cure for cancer – whatever."

I keep signing. "You make it sound hopeless."

"It is hopeless. The thing to understand, Victor, is that the world is the way it is because the world is the way it has to be."

"That's a simple tautology. It carries no substance."

"Think again. It's the nature of the beast."

"Meaning what?"

"Meaning that the whales will eventually die off, there will always be starving children, there is no cure for cancer and humankind will continue to hack each other to bits, eat the flesh and boil the bones for soup. There is no escaping what is natural to the human species in particular and to the planet at large."

"Not everyone behaves this way."

"No. But the vast majority do. And these are the ones we appeal to – the lowest common denominator, the herd mentality, the mass consumer who is content to maintain the status quo even as civilization crumbles around them. Why should they care, since they have no concept beyond themselves and maybe, possibly, their immediate families, anyway? We provide them with heroes, with celebrities, and this makes them happy. Or, at least, happy enough."

"And you believe this?"

"It doesn't matter what I believe. My advice to you? Spend whatever time you have in the manner that suits you."

"Because, in the end, *momento mori: remember that you must die.*"

"You along with Byron, Paris, Tom and Homer, sharing the same shovel full of common dirt. *Satis verborum: no more need be said.*"

"What happens now? How do I know this isn't one of those contracts where every wish is followed by disaster or death?"

"As in a pact with the Devil? Or as in the story of *The Monkey's Paw*, the son called back from the dead by his parents, only to appear before them as he was at the time of his tragic death – dragged through the cutting machine?" The woman laughs. "Don't be so melodramatic, Victor. That's the stuff of urban legends and has no basis in fact. We have no control over how you die, only how you live."

"Yeah? I suppose that maniac who shot at me is also an urban legend."

"That was for effect. Pure theatrics. Consider the threat ended." She snaps her fingers. "Poof! You are free to reclaim your life."

"Uh-huh. And all those things I said..."

"Not to worry. The public loves to see that those they look up to have feet of clay and are only *human all too human*. It makes their own faults and problems appear minuscule in comparison. The main thing is: admit, repent, reform. Don't worry, our people will be in contact and they'll guide you through the process." She grinds her Colt into the carpet with her shoe. She catches me staring, my jaw likely dropped.

"Someone is paid to clean the carpet, Victor. Someone else is paid to replace it. We're part of the cycle. It's our job to keep the machinery running. There is no other. Better get used to it."

She packs the papers into her briefcase.

"One more question."

"What is it?"

"Your name?"

"It's irrelevant, I told you."

"Maybe, but I need to know. Is it like, Lucy or Luciana? First or last name? Maiden name or married?"

She shakes her head and hands me a business card. The name reads: Sarah Tanner, a lawyer for the firm Bennett, Boggs & Fox.

Sonofabitch, I think.

"My ex-wife is a lawyer for this firm. Do you know her? Susan Murdoch. Though you might recognize her as Maja, she changed it a while back."

"No. It's a large firm and I was only brought on board temporarily." She gets to the door and turns her head. "Feel free to stay. You have the room until four this afternoon. Order in lunch. Help yourself to anything. It's all been taken care of."

"Good. Thanks. I can't really go back to my apartment yet, anyway. The window was shattered."

"It's been repaired. Take care, Victor. Goodbye. Don't forget to floss."

Right. I pour another shot into my glass and ponder the card. Sarah Tanner. Again with the soft ending name, *Sarah*. Is there a connection?

Lucian...Luciano...Lucia...Sarah... Lucia/Sarah? No. Not nearly close enough. Sarah Tanner. Sarah Tanner, I repeat. Hey, wait a gall-darned second here... Sarah Tanner? If I take the first two letters from Sarah and the first three letters from Tanner I get... SATAN! Satan... LUCIFER!

Luciano/Lucian/Lucia...LUCIFER!

The ghost in the machine.

9

Over a year has slipped past. But, *boyohboy*, what a year! My movie, *Deadly Highway* (formally *The Long Drive Home*), was nominated for best picture at the Academy Awards. It didn't win, though Ben took home the Oscar for best actor while Salma grabbed the trophy for best supporting actress. Everyone was very pleased, overall, and it was a great party full of beautiful, beautiful people. Not just *physically* beautiful, which is a given – those bodies, those outfits, those jewels! (even me looking pretty darn spiffy in Armani) – but deep down inside; where it counts. I mean it. Ben is really a sweet guy when you get to know him, with tons of personality and, let me tell you, if he was ever on the wrong side of a bottle or did drugs or had anything going on with Matt *bedroom-wise*, you couldn't tell by me. And Salma! Salma has a terrific sense of humour and is really quite the hard-working, dedicated, no-nonsense, clever, down-to-earth girl. In fact, she offered me her own special recipe for salsa verde, if you can believe it.

What a sweetheart!

My second novel came out in the spring, a six-hundred-and-fifty-page epic titled *As Good As Dead*, about a young man of humble beginnings, conceived by a bona fide Cree Indian, cancer-filled mother who dies giving birth to her son in rural Saskatchewan. The young man is subsequently raised, for a time, by his black, French-Canadian, strict, alcoholic, slightly demented, God-fearing, Baptist father who subsequently goes out of his mind (partially from grief at the loss of his wife, partially from living the tough life of a farmer on the prairies, partially due to the fact that his son is a hermaphrodite and where does that fit in God's plan?) completely, and is sent off to perish in a home for the mentally ill in Weyburn while the son is placed in a foster home. Having managed to survive the atrocities of the foster home (the novel presents more elaborate detail, including beatings, whippings and sexual abuse), our hero then moves to Djakarta where he loses a leg in the mountains while involved in an orgiastic, drugged-up religious ceremony gone very wrong, then proceeds to return to Canada to live in a primarily Italian section of Toronto.

The story goes on to tell of the challenges he faces trying to find employment as an actor *slash* massage therapist in the big city especially in terms of his mixed cultural background and anguish over his ambiguous sexual identity, particularly when he falls hopelessly in love with a creature he claims is half chicken, half human, which he claims he discovered living inside the sewer system and which he claims speaks to him via the toilet and which he believes to be the physical incarnation of a certain Asian pagan deity that has followed him across the ocean by assuming one totemistic form after another.

Meanwhile, further outbreaks of bird flu are stretching their wings (so to speak) to North America and where does that place our hero, exactly, with his chicken/human love object, even as humans are infected and die and hundreds of thousands of birds are being garrotted and tossed unceremoniously into makeshift incinerators?

Sounds pretty intriguing so far, yes? And we haven't even got to the part about the gay, alien cannibals who ride robotic horses and speak like John Wayne on speed. Talk about your major gender-bending, genre-breaking novel!

I mean, who dreams up these things?

I wasn't too crazy about the title they chose, at first. A touch too sombre, I thought, but I can't argue the results – the book virtually leapt off the shelves and is well into its twelfth printing to the point I've gown pretty used to it and feeling quite comfortable. And the money doesn't hurt either, ha ha. To be honest, I haven't had a chance to read the book yet, personally, I've been so busy with the media circus. Just kidding about the circus bit. I love these guys, and, to tell the truth, all reports so far make the novel sound pretty darned exciting and a heck of a good read. A real page-turner! Here's just a sampling of the reviews so far:

"A compulsively readable, brilliant novel, an astonishingly original work of fiction."

"A brilliant amalgam of fantasy and interior monologue, and its Melvillian manner will confirm Stone's status as a most compelling writer."

"Bizarre, charming and captivating... This elegant and sharply written novel left this reviewer speechless. A masterpiece."

"This is truly the Great Canadian Novel. As Good As Dead emerges as Stone's most touching, most emotionally accessible book to date."

The same folks who put together *As Good As Dead* are currently working on my next novel and they'll be sending me the Coles Notes version any day now to have a gander. I told them I like to be involved at a base level; sort of keep my hand in, y'know?

They're a swell group of folks and agreed totally and said it was only *fair dinkum* and *kosher* to keep me posted.

Fair dinkum and kosher. I love that sort of talk. It's so down to earth while simultaneously being sort of sexy and multicultural. I mean, these guys cover all the bases. What a terrific bunch, eh? No problem with egos here, no siree. It's all about the integrity of the work.

Of course, again, the money ain't bad either, ha ha.

Things are truly excellent and moving along on a fast and even keel.

Also, I've cut back on the red meat, eliminated the rotgut booze (nothing but the best from here on in for this cowboy), I go to the gym and work out five days a week, I have my own personal trainer, I've taken up jogging and enlisted a Pilates coach. The shaggy beard look is gone, I floss eight to ten times a day and the difference shows in my smile. I've never looked or felt better or been in better shape – though I am considering getting a hair transplant, a chin lift, a tummy tuck and maybe a nose job sometime in the near future. I have the name of an excellent plastic surgeon given to me by someone in the biz who prefers to remain anonymous, but whose initials are C-H-E-R. Meanwhile, my team of expert agents, promoters and business managers have me doing a megabucks watch ad in Switzerland, a Scotch ad in Tokyo and there's some discussion about starting up a Victor Stone clothing line. Maybe even a men's cologne. I have become so much *Lost In Translation* as we like to say in Tinseltown, and a very hot, hippity-hop commodity.

"I've got the world on a string, wrapped around my finger."

Well, praise the Lord and pass the ammunition! Oh, that's right, I've also picked up on a little old-time religion. Nothing too over-the-top; just the basics; enough to cover all the popular territory. I figure, if there is a God and a heaven after earth, I might as well be prepared. And if there isn't, what's it cost me? Nada. Besides, everyone who's anyone is into something these days and you've gotta keep *up* if you want to stay *in*, get my drift?

So, I've lately been checking into the kabbalah. Demi gave me the traditional red string bracelet I'm wearing. Sweet.

I'm also considering adopting a child. Maybe two. Why not? Everybody's into it these days and I don't want to be left behind. I just have to decide on a country of origin. Some place exotic, though not *too-too*, you know what I mean? I've been doing the conflab with Angie. She knows the ins and outs and even gave me an A-list of qualified nannies. What a doll!

Oh, excuse me, that's my cellphone.

"Hi, Mom? Yeah, I'm just taking the Beemer for a spin up Mountain Highway. It's a beautiful day, I've got the top down, and I'm taking in the sights. Yeah, I remember. And if I didn't, it's punched into my BlackBerry, or, my *CrackBerry*, as we like to say, ha ha! Dinner at eight, and don't be late. No, I won't be bringing the same girl with me as last time. Yeah, I know she was nice, but it didn't work out. Don't worry, you'll love the girl I'm bringing. She's a screenplay writer. Or wants to be, I can't remember. Right. Whatever. See you."

Yeah, as you've probably guessed, I've relocated to the beautiful *Wet* Coast. Bought myself a big, sweet hacienda in North Vancouver with a brilliant view and a sparkling swimming pool. My sister came by and sold me a hot tub – the most expensive one they had – no kidding! What a smooth talker, ha ha! Of course, I also own a sweet piece of property on the beach at Malibu and I've leased a sweet apartment in the Big Apple – New York, New York – a place so nice they had to name it twice, ha ha!

But it's not all fun and games; not by a long shot. I've taken on the role of poster boy for Friends of the Ecology (now simply Friends of Ecology, my idea so as to be known strictly as FOE. Our slogan? BE FRIENDS WITH FOE! Also my idea. Pretty neat, eh? And catchy). There was a meeting this morning and there's a fundraiser tomorrow night at the Pan Pacific, very swish and *la-di-dah, donchyaknow*. We're going tooth and nail after those companies involved with the development, promotion and production of genetically-modified foods. It's a huge undertaking that will involve tons of funds on the part of many and tons of time on my part, what with hooking up with individual and corporate sponsors and planning media blitzes. Then there's the travel involved. This thing has really become a global issue. Studies have shown that there may not be a kernel of corn anywhere in the world that hasn't been tainted in some one way, shape, form or another.

Pretty depressing when you think about it.

The good news is that I'll be visiting France next week to check out the local farms. The weather should be gorgeous and the French countryside is *trés belle*. I'll be going with the new executive director of FOE, Lena Lawson. I helped hire her (specifically because she's a babe and her initials are L.L., like in the *Superman* comic) and we've got a bit of a thing going on, so it'll be fun to mix business with pleasure.

I'm also looking forward to checking out the local vineyards and shipping back a few cases of fine wine on the company dime (one of the perks of being president of the board for a not-for-profit charitable foundation as they're not allowed to pay me a salary for my contribution, so...) It all works out in the end – I scratch your back, you scratch mine, and so on and so forth.

As you can imagine, I don't have a lot of time for my own work and I've had to put the writing of my book of poems on the back burner. Maybe give it a shot in the winter. I take some satisfaction knowing that the time is spent working for a bigger cause.

Well, I've got to fly. I'm meeting a young female student reporter from Douglas College. She wants to interview me over drinks at my place around the pool and in the hot tub. Shouldn't take long. The interview part, I mean. My people have already answered her questions and this is simply a formality: attach a face and a personality to the data.

Anything I can do to help someone along with their *education*, I say.

Oh, by the way, if anyone out there in readership land is interested in donating to a worthy cause, check out our Web site. Or Google me personally. I'd be only too pleased to take your money, ha ha!

Just kidding!

What did Freud say, again? Semohitng aobut fmae, foturne and buetaiufl leovrs?

Let me tell you something: he didn't know Jack.

That's a joke, ha ha!

Zoom, zoom, zoom...

Speaking of dignity, thanks for the job in the circus. It was fun and there wasn't much to do.
– from the novel *Hopscotch* by JULIO CORTAZAR

ACKNOWLEDGEMENTS

To Mike O'Connor, whose initial encouragement kick-started my perilled, fictive course (and, more particularly, this novel). To my family, whose lives I've borrowed and altered to suit my own deviltry – forgive me. Also, love to Jacquie, who accepts it all with a sense of humour, and so helps keeps the wheels from falling off.

Thanks to Beth Follett, Ken Sparling and Zab at Pedlar Press, for their acceptance and fine assistance. As well, to the OAC Writers' Reserve Program and the Toronto Arts Council, for their financial support.

Chapter 7 was first published in "Anthology X," Montreal.

STAN ROGAL was born in Vancouver and now resides in Toronto. His work has appeared in numerous literary journals and anthologies in Canada, the US and Europe. He has published fourteen books, including two novels, three short story and nine poetry collections, the most recent being *Fabulous Freaks* from Wolsak and Wynn. His plays have been produced variously across Canada.

OD AS GOOD AS DEAD AS G
S GOOD AS DEAD AS GOOD
AD AS DEAD AS GOOD AS D
S DEAD AS GOOD AS DEAD
OD AS GOOD AS DEAD AS G
S GOOD AS DEAD AS GOOD
AD AS DEAD AS GOOD AS D
S DEAD AS GOOD AS DEAD
OD AS GOOD AS DEAD AS G
S GOOD AS DEAD AS GOOD
AD AS DEAD AS GOOD AS D
S DEAD AS GOOD AS DEAD
OD AS GOOD AS DEAD AS G
S GOOD AS DEAD AS GOOD
AD AS DEAD AS GOOD AS D
DEAD AS GOOD AS DEAD A
OD AS GOOD AS DEAD AS G
GOOD AS DEAD AS GOOD
D AS DEAD AS GOOD AS D
DEAD AS GOOD AS DEAD A
DAS GOOD AS DEAD AS GO
GOOD AS DEAD AS GOOD A